C000220711

END
PO\NT

PETER BREAKSPEAR

Matador
9 Priory Business Park,
Wistow Road, Kibworth Beauchamp,
Leicestershire. LE8 0RX
Tel: 0116 279 2299
Email: books@troubador.co.uk
Web: www.troubador.co.uk/matador
Twitter: @matadorbooks

ISBN 978 1785892 622

British Library Cataloguing in Publication Data.
A catalogue record for this book is available from the British Library.

Printed and bound by CPI Group (UK) Ltd, Croydon, CR0 4YY
Typeset in 11pt Aldine401 BT by Troubador Publishing Ltd, Leicester, UK

Matador is an imprint of Troubador Publishing Ltd

To my wife, who has always been there for me.

1.

It was dark and the weather was getting worse; horizontal rain and colder by the minute. At least the special clothing they had been issued with was suitable for the task. The three men had been sent out to recover the item that had fallen to Earth the day before. None of them even knew for sure what they were looking for but all knew that it had to be retrieved or there would be serious consequences. At the briefing they had all been told that failure was not an idea any of them should have. All three were now standing against a large rocky outcrop at the top of the escarpment and were able to look down into the valley – not that they could see much with the weather.

Tom, who was the lead, had to make a decision or they would be at this all night. A muscular man who had a certain presence about him, he was the sort of man who could be in the background and go largely unnoticed but as soon as he moved into the area of conversation he had the natural ability to take control. It wasn't obvious where he came from as he had an almost flat, non-regional accent that had come from years working in the military or with the military on many assignments around the world. He could get by in half a dozen European languages, was almost fluent in Arabic, and was very capable in most of the central Asian dialects.

'OK fellas, let's go down the incline over by the rail.'

The rail he referred to was a long rusty metal pipe that seemed to come out of the rock and disappear over the edge of the path. It was probably something to do with the old mining industry that had long since vanished from these parts. Next to the rail, as it went over the edge from the pathway, a large amount of disturbed earth could be made out in the gloom. *It appears that we are not the first to come this way today,* Tom thought. It wouldn't be the first time that teams had been doubled up on jobs like this.

'Warning, boss.' The comment had come from the last person in the group, a small man called John who was looking at the radiation warning device that was attached to his forearm; it was designed to indicate several types of radiation that were in the area. The light on it was flashing.

'Where from and how much?' asked the leader.

'Seemed to come from down there, but it has gone now, maybe a glitch.'

'Maybe but did you get any indication of type?'

'I did but it isn't likely,' John said looking at the device that had warned them.

'What do you mean?' Tom was getting irritated now; all he wanted were the facts and no comment.

'X-ray,' John said, still unconvinced that it could be.

'Was the dosage critical?' asked Tom.

'No, way down and only lasted half a second.' He cancelled the warning and looked up, ready to proceed.

'Let's go,' Tom said indicating with his arm that the other two in the team were to follow.

The three men started down the incline and immediately noticed that not only was the going very slippery but there had indeed been someone down the slope before them. The track was very churned up and very wet. It took nearly twenty minutes to reach the bottom by which time all three were breathing hard and covered in mud from the many slips and slides that had occurred.

The rain had now eased and the wind was less severe, probably because they were now in the lee of the valley wall so were sheltered from the worst of the weather.

'Warning, boss.' John was looking at the meter on his arm. 'Same as last time: low-level X-ray for a couple of seconds, coming from that way.' He pointed in the direction they were going.

'This is weird!' Tom said. 'Why are we getting X-rays here?'

The other two men didn't answer but they too were thinking the same. In all the simulations and practices they had undergone for this mission X-rays had never been mentioned. Everything from microwaves to gamma radiation had been talked about as a likely finding, but not X-rays.

'Maybe the sensor is on the fritz,' remarked the third man. He was unusually tall, about six-foot eight and very muscular, just the sort of help you would need if things went pear-shaped. His name was David but was universally known as Big Dave, a very reliable member of the team who very rarely complained or even made a comment that was not needed. He had proved his worth over countless engagements with all manner of enemies across the world; very confident and extremely capable but was certainly not a taker of undue risks.

'It was tested and calibrated nearly to death before we got it, so it should be fine,' said Tom. 'Anyway, we are here now and the thing is warning us; let's take it at face value and do what we are supposed to do.'

What they were supposed to do was determine the level and intensity of any radiation and, if they were lucky, get a direction from which it was coming. At the moment it was only short bursts of X-ray and at levels that were not a danger.

It was aware of them, of course; it had become aware when they were on the upper level. It was now curious as to what they would do now they were this close. The short scans it had initiated had probably alerted them to its presence but that didn't matter too much. At least it knew that they carried nothing that could damage it. They were not a threat.

The three men spread out across the narrow road that ran the whole length of the valley. It was mainly used by the hill farmers moving livestock and equipment around and was beginning to show the wear and tear that had taken place over many years of use.

'We will go down the hill on the road as there is no point dragging our arses through the mud and crap that sits on either side; it will be quicker and we can all go home and have a kip. Keep your eyes and ears open and let's not get surprised by anything.'

Tom set off, walking in the middle of the road; John and Big Dave, a short distance behind and on opposite sides, kept a watch left and right – something they had gotten used to over the time they had been part of the Special Task Team. The STT had attracted a lot of interest from the rest of the unit but any information as to what they did was restricted to a need-to-know basis. It actually wasn't that difficult to work out what the STT did; the clue was in the name. They were a team that did special tasks. Simple! They also got paid a shed load of money for their efforts but that was only right considering the dangers they often faced.

'Warning, boss, same as last time, very low level but continuous now.'

'Where from?' asked Tom.

'It seems to be coming from just in front of you,' John said looking at the instrument.

It was seeing them very clearly now; they were very close

but didn't seem to have noticed its presence. It was scanning them trying to determine how they were constructed and if it had missed anything from its first look at the three individuals. All three were of a different size; it found this a little puzzling, they were all the same but all different. It stopped scanning.

'Gone now, no output at all. I'm still not convinced this thing is working properly.'

The group started moving again; with any luck they would soon arrive at the end of this part of the search area and have a break. There were probably several teams in this valley all looking for the same thing, whatever it was.

'Warning: five seconds, X-rays.'

They were very close to it now and still they seemed unaware of its presence. It pondered on how the three individuals perceived the world – certainly not the way that it did otherwise they would have been alerted long ago. Its instructions were clear, "Do no harm", so it waited and did nothing.

'Gone again – I'm now sure this thing's knackered, boss.' *Should have brought another one,* John thought.

'Never mind that now, let's get this done.' Tom started moving forwards again and the others followed.

'Behind us now, only a quick burst but much higher output, almost into the red.'

'I really do hope that thing is broken or we are having some serious stuff going on here and I cannot imagine what it could be.' Tom had stopped when John had given the warning and was now looking back up the road the way they had come.

The team had been briefed that the object they were searching for was more than likely to emit a radiation signature at varying wavelengths but had been given no real idea of what or how long or how varied it would be. The only thing they had detected was X-ray and what was that about? Broken equipment? Some sort of background anomaly? Or actual X-rays being directed at them?

The rain was still falling; a light but persistent rain that would make you very wet, very quickly. The three men had spent hours, if not days in this sort of weather over the last week. Still, the clothing they had was proof against the worst of it.

Tom was now unsure what to do; go back the way they had come and try and determine what the X-ray source was, or accept that the detector was malfunctioning and move on? The target may well be behind them and the radiation source, if real, was indicating that. Or if the sensor was indeed giving out random warnings they could waste all evening chasing ghosts. The first warning was received up on the escarpment and it indicated that the source was down here in the valley. After that, a couple of warnings that it was closer and just now, one that had indicated they had gone past it.

'I reckon that if this indication is real, the source cannot be more than a hundred metres from here and behind us,' Tom said, trying to convince himself.

'We walked past it then?' asked John

'Tell you what, I will backtrack down the road awhile and you two stay here with John keeping an eye on the sensor. If you see any indication or high levels going on give me a shout on the IC.' Big Dave was adjusting his communication set so that the earpiece didn't cause any more discomfort than it already was.

'Good idea, Dave, but do not go more than a hundred metres or so and give us a talk through,' Tom ordered.

Big Dave put his rucksack down on the ground and adjusted his webbing so that his personal weapon, the XT, was more comfortable across his chest. The XT was experimental and had been designed to give maximum knock-down effect without completely destroying the target. If you hit a person you would not kill them but you would seriously ruin their day. It had been designed around the old taser-type weapon that connected the target with 50,000 volts. Few people could stand that but some could. The XT was a few generations beyond that. It didn't need to be connected to the target but would emit pulses of high voltage that increased in intensity and current for as long as the firer decided it should. So a compliant target would get a nasty shock but a non-compliant could end up cooking themselves.

'Won't be long,' Big Dave said cheerfully as he loped off down the road.

It was watching the three closely now. One had separated from the group and was approaching on his own; why?

'Warning low-level X-ray again.'

'Roger that,' Dave said over the radio.

Big Dave was now out of sight but they could hear him over the open mic.

'Bugger all down here, boss. Is the warning still showing?'

'No, flat, buddy, nothing at— *Wow!* What was that?'

The sensor on John's arm had lit up like some seaside illumination and the audio alarm had triggered, meaning that the radiation level was past critical and well into the danger zone. At the same time a very brief but very bright light burst into the area in which John was standing. There was no noise just the warning from the sensor.

'Shut that thing off,' snapped Tom looking down the road to where Dave must be.

'Dave, can you hear me?' Tom spoke calmly into the microphone, wishing that Dave would respond. *This is going belly up,* he thought to himself.

'Right, what are the levels now?' Tom asked John.

'Back to normal, only lasted a couple of seconds. All came

from the same direction, radiation right across the spectrum; everything this thing can detect was detected.'

John was pointing down the road as if it wasn't obvious by now.

Both men had now dropped all the extra kit they were carrying and had made ready the not-inconsiderable fire power that they had with them. No electric tickling sticks now; these things were designed to kill an elephant without too much effort.

'Let's go, John, don't take chances.' Both men started to walk quickly down the road to where Big Dave had gone. He still wasn't answering the call on the radio. Tom was ready for the worst but had no idea what the worst could possibly be.

Wasn't long before they found a large scorch mark in the road; it was still steaming from the light rain that was falling. Just off to the side of the mark was the XT that Big Dave had been carrying; next to it were Dave's wet-weather gear and his belt with his radio and torch attached to it. There was no sign of Dave.

'Have a look over there, John. I will have a look into this ditch. Don't get too far from me.' They both looked around the immediate area for about twenty minutes and found nothing.

Tom went over and picked up the XT; it was warm as if it had been recently discharged.

'Have a look at the settings on this thing.' Tom beckoned to John.

'Blimey, it is set at maximum, you could zap a dinosaur with that and it has been discharged. What was he shooting at? This is getting too big for us, boss,' John remarked looking very distracted.

'You're right, it will be light in an hour or so and the weather seems to be easing off so we are going to tab it down the road, retrieve our kit and check in with control.'

Tom knew now that it had been a big mistake not to bring with them the rear-link radio kit; right now it would have been very useful but the team had followed procedure and only brought the very short-range personal stuff. The reasoning being that they had clear orders and had a limited task; why advertise their presence with radio transmissions booming out over the airwaves? No, it was the right decision at the time but was now a little flawed. Tom was already walking briskly the way they had come and John was very close behind.

It was aware that they were moving away but did not fully understand what had just transpired. A single one had come very close to it but had not seemed to have recognised it or not thought it was a threat, which of course it wasn't; well, not under normal circumstances.

It had detected a very large burst of power from the weapon the one was carrying then a large discharge of light, then nothing. Was it something it had done? It didn't think so but couldn't be sure. The other two had then come down the road; it could sense that they were very agitated but they posed no threat. They had moved around the area then had departed taking the weapon that was on the floor with them. The one that had arrived first had not been evident after the burst of light. It thought about that for a while. Was it in any danger? No; only two more rotations. It waited.

Tom and John, having retrieved theirs and Big Dave's kit, were moving at best speed up the road and onto the track that would take them to the rendezvous point up on the side of the valley. They were moving tactically but making good time all the same. Whatever had happened to Dave was not going to happen to them, not if they could help it.

It was nearly half an hour of hard flog before they reached the top of the valley. They could see the dimmed light marking what was to be the meeting point and help.

'Big Dave is missing but otherwise no damage or lost equipment.' Tom was briefing his boss by the side of a large truck that was parked near the exit point from the valley. The rain by this time had eased considerably and the predicted storm had not yet materialised, which would make any further work in the valley a little easier.

Joe Brunt, the man from control, was listening intently as Tom described the entry to and from the area they were interested in.

'What were the readings on the sensor at the time Dave left us?' Joe said making notes on a palmtop, which was transmitting as he wrote to the base area some hundreds of miles away.

'Off the scale, but only for a couple of seconds then back down to nothing. No residual, nothing, never seen anything like it.'

'Only X-rays?'

'Yes, except when Big Dave went, then it was right across the spectrum. John is downloading the log now.'

'And there was no sign of Dave after this?' Joe continued writing.

'No, nothing, only the XT lying on the ground; it had been discharged at maximum.'

'OK, mate, get yourself and John onto the transport, your job here is done.'

'Are we not getting more people down there to look for Dave?' Tom asked rather puzzled.

'Yes we are, but you are not, get on the truck and have a rest and a brew.'

Tom picked up his kit and wandered over to John who was just completing his debrief.

'Come on, mate, we're done here.'

'What about Big Dave?'

'Someone else's problem; don't worry, they will look for him.'

Although the group on the top of the valley was hidden from it by the escarpment, the entity could count that there were no more than fifty individuals up there. They did not seem to be moving towards it at this time. It waited and watched.

'I think we have it.' Joe was talking to a man who had been in the background during the debriefs. He was now standing very close to Joe so as not to let their conversation be overheard by anyone else.

'Could be but let's not be too confident; we have more to do before we can relax on this one,' the man said.

2.

It had all started some years ago when at 03:30 hours on the 21st June 2010 the Swift spacecraft had been hit with a massive burst of X-rays; the blast was at such a magnitude that the vehicle's sensor array was completely overwhelmed. The data that was downloaded as the burst was in progress also confused the software that was in use in the ground station. The software could not determine what had happened or provide a realistic analysis of the data received in the short time the sensor array on the vehicle had been active. X-rays arrive in our solar system all the time but nothing on this scale; previously the brightest X-ray source had been from a neutron star called Scorpius X-1, which sits 9,000 light years away. This recent burst had been fifteen times the magnitude of Scorpius X-1 and had originated some five billion light years away. The level of radiation posed no danger to the Earth because X-rays are absorbed by the atmosphere but lengthy repairs were required on the Swift vehicle, which was in a geostationary orbit 600 kilometres out.

Gamma ray and X-ray bursts, such as this one, were thought to originate from collapsing stars when matter is ejected almost at the speed of light. This huge burst was no exception as a massive level of gamma rays was detected at the same time.

The radiation detected would have left its start point about half a billion years before the Earth was formed, or at least that is what the laws of physics indicated at the time.

It had only been a couple of days before the X-ray phenomenon became apparent. They were turning up all over the place but in very low-level short bursts. Most of the scientific community came to the conclusion that it was more background radiation originating from space until a team from the Russian Space Federation determined that the X-ray burst was coming from a point in space about 450,000 kilometres away, just outside the orbital path of the Moon.

It had been difficult to say exactly where the point of origin was but it seemed to move in and out of a line drawn from the Moon to Earth; that is it seemed to be "hiding" behind the Moon and only appeared as the Moon came closer or moved way from Earth during its orbit. Scientists from other countries had initially scoffed at the Russian claim saying that there was absolutely no way that the recent X-ray source could be coming from that point but the evidence was beginning to stack up.

It was soon agreed that the source was emitting a constant stream of X-rays and only the movement of the Moon in relation to it was giving the impression of bursts. So the point of origin for this radiation was somewhere behind the Moon that was slightly out of sync with the Moon's elliptical orbit but was itself in orbit; not only around the Earth but also in orbit around the Sun.

The whole thing had been put onto the back burner after that with little money and even less effort being expended on the anomaly. The X-ray source should have been fully investigated; that had now become clear.

It was again the Russians who made the next step; they had realigned some scientific instruments that had been part of the Lunokhod programme, a lunar rover experiment that had seen several vehicles placed on different parts of the Moon. One particular rover had been on the far side of the Moon for some years. They were looking for evidence of water that would enable prolonged manned missions in the future. The data had been collected and the rovers switched off until now.

Rover 2001 had been reactivated and instructed to point its receiver antenna skywards. The antenna was designed to receive information on ground stations at various points on the Moon's surface and then retransmit the information back to Earth via several more ground "nodes" placed on the surface.

At first, nothing out of the ordinary was detected but, during week three of the sweep, a weak X-ray source was detected. It seemed to be the thing everybody was looking for but wasn't strong enough; it was only after several days of recalibration that it was found that it was indeed the same point of origin that was noticed from Earth.

The scientific community had now reached a consensus; the X-ray source had been identified, but what next? Did it pose any problems for anybody either on Earth or in space? Most thought that although the X-ray source was intriguing it was not of any critical importance so therefore a large expenditure of cash on the problem was not warranted. The Russians, however, agreed to monitor the anomaly and report back if anything of significance was discovered.

The small team of Russians were working under a former cosmonaut called Gregor Sevarnich, a man who in any tests would score genius level without much apparent effort. He had been recruited from the military into the cosmonaut programme and had soon shown himself to be a very quick and decisive leader. He now found himself, at the age of sixty-four, in charge of a major project with minor project funding.

Despite the feeling that he had been pushed into a task

that he would not enjoy, he applied himself with his normal overcooked drive for the job in hand.

'First we shall try and get a "look" at this thing,' Gregor said to the assembled team that seemed to have little enthusiasm for the job with which they had been dumped. Most of them had been taken from other more important tasks but, as always, some slack had been identified and they were it.

The vehicle on the Moon had a camera that had been used quite extensively to help the rover navigate around close-in obstacles such as large outcrops of rock or deep holes that would hinder the rover's progress or if the hole was deep termination. They would now have to try and reactivate the camera and attempt to point it skywards and try and get a reasonable image of the target. The zoom on the camera was not what Gregor would have wanted but the imaging device was able to give quite a high resolution. With any luck they would be able to see what, if anything, was there. They already knew that they had detected something outside of the visible spectrum but now they would determine if anything in the visible could be found.

Fortunately the vehicle did not need to move any great distance; it had already travelled most of the required distance when they were looking for the X-ray source so it was within a few hundred metres of the best point.

Because of the distance of the Moon to the Earth any commands sent or received would not be in real time; there would be around a two-second delay so what the team would see on the monitor would have happened at least two seconds ago and any instructions they sent to the vehicle would not happen for another two seconds. A further delay would be encountered as the signal was transferred through the fibre optic and microwave connections on the Moon. Great care had to be taken and any commands for movement assessed against all the possible obstacles that lay in the rover's path.

'I think that we should keep on the present heading and move in a straight line to the corner of that feature.' Vladich, a man in his twenties, was pointing at the screen indicating a large boulder that sat about fifty metres from the camera.

'OK, let's get a range to it and then we can proceed,' Gregor instructed him leaning over his shoulder.

'Fifty-two metres.' Vladich had instructed the laser rangefinder mounted on the vehicle to fire at the boulder.

'Let's not take any chances; move the rover forwards forty metres on this heading and then retake the range, we don't want to find that the laser is giving incorrect returns at this stage.'

Vladich was typing in the instructions on his keyboard and with a last look at his boss pressed the execute key.

The delay seemed much longer than four seconds but the terrain suddenly moved as the rover edged forwards the forty metres and then stopped.

'Lase it again,' Gregor said still leaning over Vladich's shoulder.

'Just over eleven metres.'

'Excellent! But we will do that every time there is any sort of obstacle that we might bump into or fall in,' Gregor instructed, happy that at least the rangefinder was working. It hadn't been used for a couple of years.

'Right, another hundred metres at forty-five degrees from here and we should be in a position to re-orientate the camera.'

The rover was now moving again having executed a forty-five degree turn; it would soon be in position.

Gregor was quite proud that after such a time the Russian technology was still working in such a hostile environment.

The rover was now halted in what had been determined as the best place for a look into space for the anomaly. A great deal of time had been spent shuffling numbers so that the rover was directly under the point that was emitting X-rays; the ideal place and the closest they were going to get without sending a spacecraft to it. The cost for that would never be sanctioned.

'So, let us now see if we can point the camera towards this thing.' Gregor was typing in commands to the rover and after a short delay the field of view on the screens changed as the camera angle moved so that it was near vertical. The scene changed from the grey lunar landscape to one of blackness.

'That will need some adjustment to be able to see anything more than black.' The comment came from an engineer called Pavlov, a small, wiry man with very bad skin. His friends joked that he looked the way he did because he had spent most of his waking life in front of a computer screen and had never been outside. He was now adjusting the gain and resolution of the incoming signal from the camera. Soon stars began to appear but not much else.

'Well, we are looking directly at it,' Pavlov said, the rest of the team also looking at the screen.

'I want you to adjust the colour threshold from black and white all the way to full colour and see what we get,' instructed Gregor.

Pavlov was busy with the controls again but because of the time delay for the signals to and fro from the vehicle it seemed to be taking ages.

'OK, we have gone through the whole range but seen nothing; let us do it an increment at a time and wait between increments; perhaps we are missing something because the transit time is too short.'

Pavlov set the adjustment interval to fifteen seconds so that the colour change would pause to enable a more detailed analysis. The process was about halfway through when Pavlov let out a low whistle.

'And what is that?' he said not quite believing what he was looking at.

It was not a clear picture of anything but rather an empty space that was not always empty. It seemed to split into several images then reform into one as if it were two liquids being mixed except that it was a continuous process. As the image moved around, the stars behind it would disappear then reappear; the process didn't seem to be repeating itself but appeared to be random.

'Could it be a problem with the data transfer?' Gregor was not convinced this was anything to get excited about. 'Move the camera completely off target and look at something we know is not moving.'

Pavlov operated the control and after a pause the image began to move; the swirling effect moved to the side of the screen then disappeared completely as the camera panned along.

'OK, hold it there and go through the whole colour range from start to end and let us see if we can get the swirling back.'

The image was changing as instructed with the true colour fading right down to grey scale and back again. There was no swirling.

'Back onto target area and see if we can get it again.' Gregor was now thinking about what it could possibly be – that's if it was still there, of course.

The camera responded to the commands sent and was now at the original point of interest. The swirling was still there.

'Go through the whole colour range again and see if that makes a difference.'

It did as before; some parts of the colour range gave a better contrast than others but the swirling was not going away.

'Make sure this is all being stored so we can have a closer

look later on. I am leaving to report all this up the chain; stay alert and let me know immediately if anything changes.' Gregor turned on his heel and left the room. He was now very interested in this but he wasn't sure what more could be done at this stage other than continue to look at the thing. He strode down the corridor and entered another office and picked up the phone.

'Gregor 4043, secure connection to the Lenin facility please.' There didn't seem to be anything happening but he knew the system was checking his voice and comparing it with several files that had been recorded over the last couple of weeks; they even recorded his voice at different times of the day and after different levels of exercise so as to get a complete record of his voice in most situations. There was a fail-safe of course; if there was any doubt he wouldn't get access, it was as simple as that.

'Lenin,' a recorded voice announced.

'Demetri,' Gregor said as clearly as he could.

'What next?' the recording said.

'Three, four, zero, four, seven, one, four, two.'

There was a ringing at the other end and a real voice answered.

'Gregor, what news?'

Gregor had no idea who the voice belonged to but knew for sure that he wasn't called Demetri as his name changed on a rotation set out by the security group. However, he was important and he was the boss.

'We have found something; we need to progress this matter to the next stage,' Gregor said into the telephone.

'Agreed, we have been watching the data, well done, Gregor.'

The line was disconnected. Gregor was surprised he had got a well done for this. A well done didn't come often and he didn't think that he had warranted special praise for something that had been not out of the ordinary. *Maybe the project is more important than it appears,* he mused.

The team would now have access to much more than at present; he could call on all sorts of agencies to assist in the work. Firstly he would need to get the October reassigned. October was a geostationary satellite that spied on other satellites and was unconventional in most ways except that it was much further out than the "ideal" distance for such a device. October was the furthest object that orbited the Earth, even further out than the Moon and was so secret that most people in the programme had thought it lost some years ago. At the moment it wasn't in a position to be of any use for this though. Not by a long way. It would have to be reassigned so that they could observe this anomaly from the other side and view it against the backdrop of the Earth and Moon.

Gregor was now in contact with the team that looked after the general day to day tasking of the satellite. He had briefed them on the situation but gave them no hint as to what they would be looking for, only that they were to reposition the satellite so as to look in the direction indicated and await further instructions. The first question had been, 'Look with what?' The October could look with many different instruments; both ends of the whole frequency band and everything in between.

He was, of course, going to look with everything at anything that they encountered; he hadn't had this much power since the giddy days of the main Mars effort some years before.

'Any changes?' Gregor was now standing behind Pavlov who was still intent on the shimmering picture on the screen.

'I don't think so but about ten minutes ago it did seem to repeat itself but on checking back with the data nothing stood out. It just seems to be totally random.'

'Are we getting any changes in the frequency output?' Gregor asked.

'No, it is still emitting low-level X-rays and some visible light but I cannot get a spectral analysis on it as it seems to be invisible to the sensor but we can see it, sort of.'

'Right, all we can do now is wait for the October to be repositioned and that will take some time. We watch and record and attempt to make some sense from all this.'

With the October in place they would be able to determine if this thing was a three-dimensional object and even if it existed where they thought it was. Gregor still had an inclining that it might not be. Perhaps it was much further away and only gave the impression that it was close. What if the October confirmed that it was an object and was where they thought it was? *More questions than answers; this was going to run and run,* thought Gregor as he watched the unchanging data displayed on the screens.

The team that controlled October was hard at work; it was a straightforward task they had been given but it would mean all their work so far would be suspended. This realignment had received the highest priority and all other work was to cease immediately. This kind of urgency had only happened once before and that was to check on what the Americans had been up to with a very large spacecraft that was behaving rather oddly. That had come to nothing but it did demonstrate to the high command that the October was in fact going to be very useful in the future. The programme had been assured and now it was on the move again.

The team had finalised the calculations and had programmed the control computer that would direct the move. All that was required now was the authority to press the commence switch and they would be moving.

3.

'Now pay attention everybody, we are about to start.' The woman speaking was a striking blonde and over six feet tall, everybody in the room was listening to what she had to say. Lily short for Nalia, her family name was Gamosk. She was usually not here at this level; it showed what importance was being placed on this to have her personally directing the operation. 'On my mark, three, two one – Commit.'

The technician pressed the "commit" button and everybody watched the screens. Nothing would happen for a few seconds as the signal had to go such a long way. They then had to wait for the return signal to tell them it was working.

'On plan,' another technician announced as the readings began to change.

'Keep your eyes open to this, gentlemen, we don't want to screw this up.' Not that they often did; in fact they had never "screwed" anything "up". But this was important, they all knew it.

'How long before stage one?' Lily asked.

'Two hours and five minutes,' a technician responded.

'Excellent, call me in an hour.' Lily turned and left the room. Everybody relaxed slightly, the immediate pressure had eased.

Out in space about 50,000 kilometres further out than the

orbit of the Moon the satellite received its instructions; a two-second burst that would send it away from its current position and put it in a more elliptical orbit, it would then be in a position to observe the point in space everybody was interested in. Nothing like this could be done with any urgency in space. All calculations of this type were checked and double-checked and only when all the errors had been identified and removed would the vehicle be instructed to move. The satellite was now on its way.

'What's this all about, Gregor?' Lily was on the phone.

'Can't say but we need the whole array to be working when October is in position,' Gregor said wishing he could tell his friend of many years what they were up to.

'It will be, Gregor, don't you worry yourself about that.' Lily said goodbye and told him he would be the first to know when the satellite was available for tasking.

It had been two hours since the October had begun to move and Lily was now back in the control room; all had gone perfectly to plan and the satellite was now very close to where it needed to be. A few more minutes and they would be there.

A link had been established between the October ground station and the Lunokhod control building; Gregor could now see what, if anything was coming from the distant October.

'In position, Gregor,' Lily said over the link. 'You can now have control of the array, hope you find what you are looking for.'

Gregor was now able to switch the main array on the satellite to whatever mode he wanted. He would try and detect the low-level X-ray that was still being received by the Moon rover. First he made sure that the uplink was working properly by sending check messages to the array on October. All was working perfectly, which didn't surprise him in the slightest.

'Have we got the X-ray signal, Serge?' Gregor was standing behind an engineer who was looking at the main control monitor.

'No – wait, yes, we have it, same level as the rover is picking up.' Gregor thought that the source was definitely transmitting in at least two directions but was probably transmitting out in all, a bit like a radio mast does on Earth.

'Not directional then?' he said aloud.

'No, sir, it seems to be acting like a beacon would with no direction except back to it.'

'So, now we are pointing right at it, let's try and get a look at it.'

Serge had entered the required instructions and the screen had lit up; at first the same indistinct jumble that had come from the rover previously but the October's equipment was several generations ahead and much more powerful than what was on the Lunokhod.

This time the image was very clear but it was not apparent what they were looking at. It was still moving around and seemed to come and go exactly as they had observed from the camera on the Moon. However, there were more colours and a little more detail, but detail of what?

'Anything other than X-rays?'

'No, nothing, sir,' replied Serge. 'It's not registering the light output but obviously we can see it.' It was the same as the information coming from the Moon. No light in the visible range detected but there was light; puzzling.

Gregor was thinking. *What if this thing is a singularity, what people often refer to as a black hole? No, not possible and not this close or we could all have been in deep trouble a while back. Showing some traits of a singularity though, X-rays emitting from it for one. No, not a black hole, certainly not the way a black hole is currently understood. Maybe a completely new and unknown phenomenon; I might even get my name attached to this one.*

They had been watching this point in space for three weeks now and people were beginning to lose interest. Already there had been calls to reassign October to more productive work. Gregor, and more importantly his bosses, had argued for the surveillance to continue but been forced to agree that this situation could not carry on indefinitely.

On day twenty-eight of the observation, Gregor was in the control room when Pavlov called him over.

'This is new, sir.' He was pointing at the main screen.

The shimmering effect had changed and was now somewhat like a smudge on the picture but the movement had stopped.

'What's it like from the other side? Get both views up next to each other.'

'Not the same anymore!' Pavlov was excited after weeks of looking at the same thing.

'Anything else emitting from it?' Gregor was now fully awake and again invading Pavlov's personal space although Pavlov was not at all aware of that; he was also peering at the screen that showed the data.

'Earth side; an increase in X-ray emissions and also low-level gamma but the other side nothing has changed.'

Even with the far more powerful sensors on the October, nothing of the increase was detected.

'That means that it is going only one way and that is towards Earth,' Gregor said more to himself than to anybody else.

'Levels are still small though, boss; nothing that would cause concern unless we were right up against it.'

The picture suddenly returned to the shimmering image and the radiation levels returned to what they had been for the last weeks. Both men stared at the screens without saying anything.

'What was that about?' Gregor said at last. 'Check the data log and let us see if it was a system glitch and not real at all.'

Pavlov was running down the information stored from the start of the change and was comparing it with all that had gone previously. 'This will take some time, sir.'

'Don't worry, Pavlov, we have enough time to get it right.'

It took Pavlov and the system nearly two hours to check and recheck the ten minutes of data to determine what, if anything was real. It was all real; the data gave the same information as they had witnessed. The anomaly had changed but only on the side facing Earth. Pavlov called Gregor on the phone and reported his findings. 'Good work, Pavlov, well done.' Gregor put the phone down and dialled the Lenin facility and after going through the security procedure spoke to the same voice as before.

'As you have been watching, sir, we have had a change in the appearance and radiation emissions from the anomaly. We are certain it was a real change and not one produced by our equipment.'

'Well done, Gregor, we are now thinking of the next step but we will keep you informed and will let you know in good time if we need you to do anything different. For now, continue monitoring.' The line went dead: end of conversation.

What Gregor didn't know for sure but had a good idea was that his superiors were busy working away with several different groups that had no direct contact with each other. Perhaps it was the Soviet paranoia that still permeated the scientific projects with Russia. Need to know basis and all that. Gregor thought it completely unnecessary but was a captive to the system.

One of the other groups was the resupply effort that was maintaining the equipment on the space station. This station had been put into orbit some time ago and was nearing the end of its useful life. It would eventually be abandoned and its orbit would decay so that it burnt up on re-entry and the remnants crashed to Earth. That wouldn't happen for some months, maybe as long as a year, but it would happen.

The resupply vehicle had been made ready to remove the last of the useful equipment from the station over the past year and was ready to launch when the anomaly appeared. The project was reassigned and new plans made; the resupply vehicle would not be going to the space station; at least not yet.

4.

The two cosmonauts were sitting in the command seats of the resupply vehicle; the countdown was in progress but it would be another hour before they lifted off. Both were experienced in the flying of the space vehicle and both had been to the space station many times before. This was going to be different, however, and they were not going to the space station; both men were looking forward to a high-profile mission, one on which they would not normally be together. Both men were commanders who would usually have a crew of three each but for now they were the whole crew. The thinking was to put all the experience available onto the flight. This was obviously being treated with some seriousness.

Flights of this nature had not quite become routine but now posed considerably less risk than when the Americans went to the Moon in the sixties and seventies. Oddly, only unmanned missions had been to the Moon since Apollo 17 was there in December 1972. The Moon was currently home to several unmanned rovers that were exploring or had explored large areas of the surface. The Russian Lunokhod was one of them. The trip to the Moon would, they both hoped, be uneventful but they both knew to take nothing for granted.

Both men were talking to the ground crew as they went

through the final checks prior to the spoken countdown. Everything was on time with no reds so far.

'All green,' the controller said over the hardwired link they had whilst they were still connected to the ground.

'All green,' Antenov repeated back to him.

Antenov had been appointed lead pilot because he was marginally more experienced and senior in rank but both of them could have easily been in command. Both were very comfortable with the other's abilities and both trusted the other absolutely.

The controller was speaking again in Russian with a slight northern Russian accent; he was from the far north and although he had been in this part of the country for most of his life he still retained the slight twang that identified his origins.

'All systems are in the green, standby for final countdown start.'

'Roger, standby for final countdown start,' Antenov repeated back.

A new voice came over the radio. 'ДЕСЯТЬ, ДЕВЯТЬ, ВОСЕМЬ, СЕМЬ.'

The voice continued in Russian; '*Six* – pressure at required level.'

'*Five.*'

'*Four* – Pre-ignition on.'

The two pilots were sitting still waiting for the massive push that would accelerate them from zero to over a hundred miles per hour in the time it took to clear the support tower. *A very expensive fairground ride*, Antenov was thinking.

'*Three* – ignition on and at full flow.'

'*Two* – pre-release activated.'

'*One* – we have separation and lift-off.'

The vehicle was now completely on internal power, they were on their own for the time being. Antenov never got used to the overwhelming exhilaration that a launch produced. The launch was going from zero to 25,000 mph and escape velocity in no time at all; as he once heard an American astronaut say, "What a ride!"

The launch drove the spacecraft at ever-increasing speeds skywards, the two crewmen were pressed very firmly into the contoured seats to such an extent that they would be unable to do anything until reaching orbit in a few minutes' time.

It took the spacecraft just under ten minutes to reach orbit but this was the start of several days of adjustment and manoeuvring. They still had much to do, not least leave orbit and attempt to get in a synchronous orbit with the anomaly on the other side of the Moon. At present they were in a stable Earth orbit and were now carrying out the necessary checks to start stage two of this endeavour in two days' time.

It had taken many conferences and much discussion to arrive at the decision to send a manned crew to the object. It was agreed without conflict. Very dangerous it may be but to put human eyes close to the target was considered the best option. The Russians were now in partnership with the Americans who were to provide an over-watch with the listening devices they had at hand. They had offered to provide both the vehicle and the crew for the mission but it wouldn't be ready for three months at the earliest. The Russians were the only ones who could do it in the short time available.

Antenov and his fellow crewman, Chekov, were now ready to begin the burn to take them out of orbit and head for the Moon. They were both aware that some years before an Apollo crew had done the same sort of procedures to enable the first man on the Moon. *Should have been a Russian,* thought Antenov.

Chekov was busying himself with the final checks that had been ordered from the ground. Once complete he nodded at Antenov and opened the communication link to the control.

'We are ready,' spoke Chekov.

'Prepare for thirty-second burn on my mark,' a voice said in their ears.

'English now, eh?'

It didn't bother either man that the transmission had switched to English; they had both been part of the joint space venture that had seen the construction of a space station and numerous satellite observatories over the past ten years. They could both switch from English to Russian and back again in mid-sentence without a pause.

'All is fine now! The Americans have arrived,' joked Chekov.

Three lights lit in turn on the main thruster panel; as the last light came on the spacecraft vibrated slightly as it was eased out of orbit, the view through the window also changed very slowly until only blackness was visible outside. They would now have to wait four days for the spacecraft to reach the position where a few minor adjustments would be made to bring it into the target area.

'Understood, sir, we will of course provide all the information we can... Yes, we will continue with the open link.' Gregor replaced the receiver; he had been talking to his boss who had informed him of the manned vehicle that was approaching the Moon. He was instructed to do nothing except observe. He wasn't sure what else he could do even if he wanted to; he was, after all, observing.

More and more people were now getting involved with the mission; it had changed when the anomaly had shifted colour and emitted higher levels of radiation a couple of days ago. Gregor had thought at the time that interest would wane and eventually he would be pulled from the project but that wasn't to be. A great many people were now fully committed on both sides of the Atlantic.

'Lily, have you been watching all this?' Gregor had called Lily to discuss the ongoing situation with the anomaly, as far as he could determine nothing had changed. *Maybe the cosmonauts will be able to get a better look when they were in position.*

'Yes, Gregor, although we haven't had anything to do since you took control; what do you think it is?'

'Don't know, originally thought it might relate to a singularity but it can't be; too close and not enough output.'

'Well it doesn't belong to anyone on Earth so all the conspiracy theories are squashed,' said Lily, joking.

'Well, Lily, we will find out soon enough when those two chaps are within touching distance in a day or so.'

'For some reason I do not envy them and I wish them luck. Bye, Gregor, speak later.'

Some time after launch the anomaly started shimmering and the radiation levels had spiked; the X-ray output had remained higher than before. Both the rover and October were now fully utilised in the observation of it. Gregor had reported the increase as soon as it became apparent; he had been told that the spacecraft was still some distance away and would not be in a position to observe for about twenty-four hours.

The increase lasted just over an hour then subsided to the previous low level.

The two cosmonauts were now approaching the anomaly but could see nothing of it. The distance would close to about ten miles, perhaps then they would be able to comment on what they could see.

The ground station director was watching the data. 'Have to be careful here,' he said to himself. The telemetry indicated that the spacecraft was now on the same orbital path as the target so would not get any closer for now.

The two cosmonauts were giving their opinion on what they could see. It seemed that they had exactly the same view as from the equipment on the Moon except they were closer and could see it with the naked eye.

'I think we will move the vehicle so that it can observe directly at the X-ray burst; that means we will put them between it and Earth.' The director was giving instructions to his team on the ground.

'Tell them what we are going to do so it doesn't take them by surprise.'

One of the engineers opened a channel to the two cosmonauts and told them what was proposed. The vehicle's structure would provide sufficient protection from the X-rays at the levels seen so far.

The engineer fed the instructions into the flight control computer and waited for the execute command from the director. 'Are we all ready?' the director asked to all around him. All were in agreement that it could now commence.

'Initiate on three: One, two, initiate.'

The engineer's finger had been hovering over the key; on "initiate" he stabbed his finger firmly down and the computer started sending the instructions to the spacecraft.

The two men out in space noticed again the slight tremor as the vehicle started to move; very slowly but it was still discernible. After three minutes the opposite thrusters fired to bring the craft to a halt; they were now in between the anomaly and Earth.

'Spiking again!' The warning came from Pavlov who had been intently monitoring the data feed from the rover. 'X-ray off the scale and high levels of gamma also.'

It all happened very quickly; as soon as the spacecraft had stopped moving the anomaly had pushed out high levels of radiation and had started to change colour; gone was the indeterminate shimmering and in its place was a very bright, nearly white, yellow that had a black centre.

The black centre grew in size until it was apparent that it had form and was coming out towards the spacecraft. The two cosmonauts stood no chance. The object that the yellow shimmering had ejected smashed into the spacecraft and carried on going. It was later estimated that the object was moving in excess of 10,000 miles per hour. It seemed to be undamaged by the collision but the spacecraft was torn to pieces and scattered into space like confetti; all of the debris tumbling around and reflecting the sunlight as it moved.

5.

Big Dave was lying on a hard floor. At least he thought it was a floor; it was difficult to determine as he was in total darkness and could see absolutely nothing. Perhaps he was blind; he wasn't sure. He couldn't hear anything either. This was like one of those sensory deprivation things that he had once tried whilst on holiday. That was a long time ago. This was similar but not the same. He couldn't detect any warm water that he might be floating in. He could feel the floor; if that was what it was. He moved his hand down from his chest to the floor to see if it was warm. Not warm but a little chilly and very smooth. He stretched out his arm and touched something just within reach; a wall perhaps, at least it went from the horizontal to the vertical as far as he could feel and it had the same smooth surface as the floor. He felt for the torch that he carried as part of the equipment he had. Not there; all the other stuff he had carried was also gone. He did a quick check; boots, combat trousers and a T-shirt – all the rest was gone; equipment, foul-weather gear…

He lay still, thinking what could have possibly happened. The last thing he remembered before waking up here was a movement off to one side then his weapon had powered up and immediately discharged into the road, then nothing. He moved his legs and neck checking he could still feel his limbs and checking they were still under command; all seemed to be well, no aches or pains and everything appeared to work except he had either been blinded or was in total darkness.

'Hello – is anybody here?'

He could hear his own voice. He tried moving his hand in front of his face to see if the darkness had any shadows in it; nothing at all. He felt all over his head and neck to see if there was any damage. His eyes felt fine, no pain, nothing; nothing that could be felt anyway.

He moved into a sitting position and leaned his back against the wall, slowed his breathing and listened; only a slight whoosh in his right ear that was always there. He was unsure if he should attempt to stand and move around; unwise he thought because he could be sat on the edge of a big drop or some other danger.

'Hands and knees,' he said aloud moving over so that he was kneeling. He leaned forwards so that his hands touched the floor and gradually moved forwards so that his nose was in contact with the floor; he took a deep breath through his nose, sniffing the floor – nothing. He quickly sniffed under his arm.

'Well that still stinks,' he said.

Being very careful that his hands remained in contact with the floor he moved forwards trying to make sure he was going in a straight line but he knew the direction would wander with the lack of visual references.

His knees were beginning to feel sore; he estimated he must have been moving for around ten minutes without encountering anything. The floor was still very flat and smooth.

He sat back and to his surprise the wall was still there. It seemed that he hadn't moved at all or the wall was following him. He was now more than a little puzzled. He sat and thought for a while.

'Perhaps I'm asleep and this is a dream,' he said aloud, raising his voice even more. 'Never had a dream where I thought I was dreaming.'

Big Dave was being observed; there were two of them watching his futile attempts to make sense of his surroundings.

'Why is it here?' one of them commented.

'It circumvented the plan and posed a danger to the next step. When it starts we will replace it back where it came,' the other replied.

'How long before start?'

'Two rotations,' the first one replied.

Down in the valley it was watching and waiting; the group up on the valley side had not moved very far from the point it first noted them. The numbers had decreased, however. It stopped scanning. Less than two rotations.

6.

'I wonder if we have a plan,' Joe muttered as he walked away from the communications vehicle. He had been on a conference call to the committee that was running the show. It had lasted over an hour with Joe giving a long and detailed explanation as to what had happened down in the valley. Everything from the known to the supposed had been discussed. It was agreed that they had indeed found what they had been looking for; but what should they do about it?

In earlier discussions everything from a nuclear strike to doing nothing had been chewed over. Hopefully it wasn't going to be the first option as this might be the last day of his and everybody else's life within a radius of ten miles.

'Still, not many people know the time and the manner of their death. I only hope they tell us before they press any buttons.' Joe was talking to himself. Of course he knew that it would not be the nuclear option because they had already found a weapon that seemed to work.

Joe had been in this position before but that had seemed to work out fine. They had found the device very quickly and had vaporised it with one of the new electrical discharge weapons that had been brought along at the start of the mission. That time it was out in the middle of nowhere in the Empty Quarter of Oman over by the Oman/Saudi Arabian border; miles and miles of nothing much. That was probably why it was referred to as the Empty Quarter. The tracking facility had followed it all the way down and the ground team had no trouble finding it. It had been giving off bursts of X-rays and sat in the open. It had taken around a week before authorisation had come to destroy it and then it was gone.

Joe remembered sitting in the desert under a very clear sky watching it; an odd-looking device about the size of a large oil drum and shiny but dull at the same time. It had resisted all attempts to discover what it was so the decision had finally been made to get rid of it. The weapon had arrived by helicopter and was set up around half a mile from the target; everyone who was not essential had been withdrawn whilst the weapon was charged; that took around two days. When they were ready, all the remaining personnel came back to the observation area. Joe remembered talking to one of the grown-ups in charge about what they expected to happen.

'We don't know. It's a bit like the very first atomic test in the States; it was thought that the nuclear reaction would set off a sympathetic reaction within the earth surrounding the test area and could possibly be the end of the planet. Didn't happen of course but a few people held their breath. Not sure what good that would have done, however.'

Joe had no idea who the man was but he was obviously in charge or at least one of the people who was running things. He was a little bit taller than Joe, maybe six-four or so; typical civilian, scruffy, a bit fat and unable to stand up straight.

Once the weapon was ready there was one last check of the surrounding area and the countdown began and, as it neared zero, there was a palpable level of fear amongst the group at the control area. "… *Three, two, one – initiate,*" came over the loudspeaker. A bright flash came from the weapon as it discharged a few billion volts and millions of amps. Nothing much else seemed to have happened. No flash from the target end, no explosion – nothing.

'Let's go and have a look then.' The clever grown-up was talking, looking round for his driver. They all piled into several vehicles and headed towards the target.

'What are the detectors saying?' the big man said to no one in particular.

'Nothing, only background; all in the green,' a technician said from the rear of the truck.

They had arrived at the point that they had shot at. The target was gone; only a mark on the desert floor and a smell of electrical discharge in the still, hot air. On that occasion that was all there was to it; mission accomplished, job done and all that. Joe had been very surprised that it had been so easy. All that effort and it was gone so quickly without any problems at all.

Joe was a little suspicious of it all; how did they know that this "Electrical Discharge Weapon" would work? They didn't seem to have tried any number of conventional weapons prior to this.

Joe didn't know that the "conventional weapons" had indeed been tried the first time one of these devices had landed. That was almost a year ago, in Siberia in the dead of winter.

It too had been found fairly easily; out in the open, on the surface and emitting what was thought to be random bursts of X-rays. It appeared to be a tube-shaped object about the size of a forty-gallon oil drum but was completely without any surface features; perfectly smooth with no visible openings or access points.

The system had moved fast on this occasion; first a Russian tank, a T-90, had been brought up. From about 500 metres away it had fired a main armament armour piercing projectile at it. The projectile had hit it perfectly in the centre of mass but had simply vanished; no penetration and no bouncing off. Next came all manner of shaped charges that were laid against the object, all resulting in nothing. The object was still there and still emitting short burst, low intensity X-rays.

The decision had finally been taken to use a low-yield nuclear device that had been developed from the American Davy Crockett Weapon System; a small nuclear device that was man portable and with a blast at the sub-kiloton level. The original Davy Crockett had been developed as a tactical nuclear weapon that would be used against the massive Soviet armour thrusts into Western Europe. It was going to be a big but not gigantic bang.

The nuclear device had been set at the required distance from the target and then fired remotely from an armoured vehicle about six miles away. The weapon had functioned perfectly with the target hidden by the flash and blast of the nuclear detonation. The only thing was that the target had survived without any visible damage. It was still in about the same place except the ground and surrounding bush were rearranged somewhat. One of two possibilities was expected; one, target destroyed or two, target thrown hundreds of feet from the detonation point. Neither had happened; not only was it bombproof but it seemed that it couldn't be moved.

At this point someone, probably a Russian, had come up with the idea of using an electrical discharge directed at the object. Both the Russians and the Americans had been experimenting with these so-called high energy discharge weapons for some years. It had taken several days to assemble the new weapon within striking distance of the object. It was determined that, even if the object was not destroyed, any internal mechanism or circuitry would be rendered inoperable.

The weapon was triggered and the result was the same as

it had been ever since; it simply disappeared and left no trace that it had ever been there. No pieces, nothing at all.

One of two things had happened it was concluded; the object had been totally destroyed or it had moved, somehow, to another place.

After this event the drive to perfect and improve the Electrical Discharge Weapon had been given a priority not seen since the development of nuclear weapons towards the end of the Second World War. How all this was kept away from the public gaze was a minor miracle in itself. What was now available was a reliable and effective counter to whatever these things were.

Joe wasn't party to all this; the only thing he knew was that this new weapon was now readily available and seemed to be on call just about anywhere in the world and now he was in a very windswept valley in Wales in the pouring rain with the first indication of dawn lighting up the valley.

'Joe!' The man in charge was shouting from behind the control truck and indicating that Joe should come closer.

'Yes, boss,' Joe said as he came around the corner of the truck. His boss was with someone that he hadn't noticed before.

'This is Doctor Jonathan Smyth from NASA in the US.' His boss said as if the NASA bit would impress.

'Pleased to meet you Doctor Smyth.' Joe said offering his hand. 'What brings you all this way on a day like this?'

'We thought that someone should be here for this one as it is somewhat different from the previous ones we have encountered.'

The doctor had said previous ones not the previous one. *Interesting*, Joe thought as he disengaged his hand.

'How many of these objects have we encountered to date?' Joe was hoping he might get a total and some more information.

'This one is different because we can't see it; the others were visible from some distance and were not that difficult to find.' The doctor ignored Joe's question.

'It would be nice if you and I could go down to the area and see the lay of the land so to speak. Is that OK with you, Joe?'

'Fine by me, Jonathan,' said Joe deliberately using the doctor's first name to try and gain a response.

'Excellent! Let's go as soon as we can.'

'Joe, keep with the doctor and give any help or advice as you see fit, remember we are still unsure as to what happened to your man down there.' Joe's boss was speaking with his back to the doctor so that the doctor was unable to overhear.

Joe picked up his kit and started towards the path that led down to the area where the object was. The doctor followed a few steps behind.

'Do we know what this thing is, Jonathan?' Joe said over his shoulder.

'Not really but has been classified as a priority one from today.' A priority one was exactly what it suggested: a number one priority to sort, overriding all other concerns and was to be pursued to the end with maximum resources.

'Why are we going down there with just the two of us then?' Joe said, thinking that they were also completely unarmed.

'So we are not perceived as a threat by the object,' the doctor said, a bit too matter-of-factly for Joe.

Joe estimated it would take around thirty minutes to reach the valley floor and a further ten to be in the area where the object was thought to be – only a little quicker than going in the opposite direction. Joe was surprised that the doctor seemed to have no difficulty in keeping up. *Not as unfit as he appears*, Joe thought.

1.

The descent into the valley was uneventful but the timing was dead on thirty minutes or so. The two men paused at the bottom to catch their breath.

'Do we know anything about this thing at all?' Joe said, hoping to gain some information about what they were really doing down here.

'Well, I don't suppose it will hurt telling you a little bit more than has been released. The whole world will soon know anyway.' The doctor paused and seemed to have his mind far away from the windswept and very wet valley in Wales. 'All started some years ago; large x-ray bursts from deep space, or at least we thought they were from deep space, then the anomaly appeared just outside the orbit of the Moon. That was tricky because the thing couldn't be where it was but somehow there it was; seemingly a moving black hole. Then these little gems started to appear.' He pointed down the valley to where the object was thought to be.

'What are they?' Joe was amazed the doctor was telling him anything at all.

'Well they all appear to be different but do the same things; the first couple could be detected in the visible spectrum and not at all difficult to find. Then this one is emitting the same sorts of radiation but is not visible across the whole spectrum. Odd, don't you think?'

Certainly is, Joe thought, but didn't say anything hoping the doctor would carry on with the narrative.

'You should now say, "What are they doing, doctor?" The doctor was now looking Joe in the eye, one eyebrow raised as if in question.

'What are they doing, doctor?'

'We don't know for sure but they seem to be scanning, if we can call it that, using what appears to be X-rays with varying intensity; goes from the very low hardly detectable to the "Let's get behind some shielding" sort of output. They then transmit, again using X-rays, back towards the anomaly the other side of the Moon.' The doctor paused. 'The X-rays go on and off without any residual radiation – none that can be detected, anyway. Then there is the situation that involved your colleague.'

'Big Dave?' Joe volunteered.

'Yes, Big Dave.' The doctor was thinking again.

'We think that the object perceived him as a threat but can't be sure, it may have been a coincidence. He was carrying a small Electrical Discharge Weapon of the type that has been successful in dealing with these things so far. Although the output from his weapon was miniscule in comparison with the one we used on the other occasions.'

'You see we have been very close to these things, even touching one, but this invisible one proved quite hard to find – your team was only one of many looking for it. Not only is it hidden but it has appeared to defend itself.'

'Are we going to deploy the large capacity gun?' Joe asked.

'No, don't think so, at least not yet.' The doctor seemed to have other things on his mind again.

'So we are going to walk up to this thing and hope for the best, are we?' Joe was getting a little agitated but did not show it.

'Yes, I think we are. If you prefer, I will go on alone but please keep within shouting distance, I would hate to disappear and no one see it.' The doctor had raised the eyebrow again. *Wish I could do that,* Joe thought for a second.

'No, we will both stay close and do this together, if this turns out to be the end of the road for me then so be it,' Joe said, not at all convinced.

'So, to recap, there have been several of these that have, maybe, come from the anomaly and all but this one have been easily detected and removed. We now have a hidden object that seems to be able to defend itself. All objects have been scanning and transmitting to the anomaly. That's about it, you now know as much as me or anyone else.'

It was watching the two individuals who had come down the side of the valley and who now stopped some way from it. It could not determine what they were doing or why they had stopped. It waited.

The two men started to walk down the road in the direction of the object, or at least to the point where they thought the object was.

It was aware of them; after a quick scan it decided that they were not a threat at this time. It waited.

Joe and the doctor had reached the point in the road that still showed the scorch mark; a puddle had formed in the middle of it, indicating that some road material had been removed when the heat was generated. Joe dipped his toe into it, gauging how much road had been removed.

'Seems to have been vaporised; about an inch down or so,' Joe said.

'What did this, do you think?' The doctor was now stood next to Joe and both were looking at the depression in the road.

'Could have been a discharge from Big Dave's weapon but

I doubt he would have just fired it at the ground; it was fully discharged when we picked it up.

It was scanning them now; no weapons that it could detect. It was unsure as to what they were doing.

The area was also being watched by others; the ones that had removed the first one were paying great interest to the two individuals that had approached the device.

'Shall I remove them?' one asked.

'No, they are no threat; if they approach with the weapon we will act, but not now.'

Joe and the doctor were still on the road; the doctor was looking into the small ditch that ran diagonally away from where they were.

'Hello, what's this then?' The doctor was pointing into the ditch. 'Something down there.'

Joe stepped into the depression and picked something up, it was a belt made from webbing, attached to it were a torch, a radio and other small items of equipment.

'This is Dave's kit, Tom said it was here.'

They laid the kit out on the road to see what was there.

'All Dave's outer clothing.' Joe was a little puzzled but tried to remain calm and objective. He had learned over many years that it was always unwise to jump to conclusions. Think before any conclusion is reached, even when the most obvious evidence is presented.

'Don't you think the clothing is a little odd?' remarked the doctor. 'The jacket and trousers are still done up, it would have been very difficult for him to remove them like that and more to the point why would he?'

'Weird!' Joe remarked, still looking around the immediate area.

'Can't see anything else; seems we have everything except Big Dave and his inner clothing.'

It was now scanning them continuously, they were very close but they seemed to be unaware.

'OK, we know it is here somewhere; let's try and find it. We cannot see it but previously it has had a physical presence.' The doctor had picked up a rock the size of a tennis ball from the side of the road.

'Not sure you could guarantee a hit even if you could see it, Jonathan.'

The doctor leant low and launched the rock in a flat trajectory on a line at right angles between them and a small clump of gorse about twenty feet away.

It had been alerted that some kind of projectiles might be directed at it but nothing as slow and simple as this.

The rock hit the object square on but only existed for an instant afterwards. It disassembled the projectile and let it drift away on the breeze.

'Did you see that?' The doctor was standing open-mouthed, looking in the direction he had thrown the rock. There had been a slight shimmer as the rock was in mid-air, then nothing.

'Seems that you did hit it first time – you should do the lottery with luck like that.'

Both men walked side by side towards the spot where the rock had disappeared; both moving slowly and with arms outstretched.

It would let them touch it.

'Well, well, I think this is it.' Joe was stopped with his hands held out seemingly feeling something.

The doctor moved over and put his hands into the area that Joe was feeling.

'Very smooth and a little warm. I wonder if this would show on thermal,' Joe said.

'We have had drones and all manner of other surveillance kit looking at the whole of this valley and not seen anything;

that's why the teams were sent in, we didn't see anything at all.

'Perhaps it can reduce the temperature to blend in with the surroundings; it seems to manage with the visible wavelengths without a problem. Perhaps it can control all radiation that is emitted; turning it on or off at will.'

The two men moved around the object to gain an idea of how big it was.

'About the size and shape of a forty-gallon oil drum, I would say, seems to be the standard size for these,' said Joe.

'Then we must assume that this is the same, or at least very similar, to the previous ones.' The doctor was making notes on his pad.

'Are we in any danger from this thing?' Joe stood away from the object but the doctor was still very close. At least Joe thought he was still close.

'Probably not, it doesn't seem to perceive us as a threat,' the doctor said, running his hands over the object again.

The two men and the object were being watched. 'Are they a threat?' one of them asked.

'No, not at this time; the device will act if it is in danger. The two individuals do not carry the weapon that has been used against us.'

It was puzzled by the two individual's actions; it could sense their thoughts but could not understand what they meant.

'What if we hit it with a rock?' Joe remarked looking round for a suitable one on the ground.

'No! We should remember what happened to the one I threw. We wouldn't want that to happen again with your hand attached to it would we?'

'No, we wouldn't.' Joe abandoned the search for a rock and stood next to the doctor.

'What's next?' Joe asked.

'We go back up and see what's to be made of all this. At least we know exactly where this thing is; that's if the drone is still up there somewhere watching us.'

The drone was indeed up there and watching, their every movement had been noted and logged; the position of the object had been determined to the inch.

It took just under an hour to retrace their steps back up the side of the valley to the control point. They arrived just as a Blackhawk helicopter flew overhead; it made a circuit of the area then landed a short distance from the vehicles.

That could have given us a lift from the valley floor, Joe thought.

'Good, the boss has arrived,' the doctor was walking towards the briefing area. 'You had better come with me, Joe; this will now involve you and your team, I expect.'

Joe followed the doctor over to a briefing marquee that Joe didn't remember from the last time he was here. It was big and set away from all the other tents and vehicles. It also had armed sentries around it. The doctor stopped at a Land Rover and spoke to a man in the passenger seat.

'This is Joseph Alan Brunt; I believe you have his pass.'

The guy eyed Joe and checked a piece of paper he had attached to a clipboard.

'Sign here,' he said, offering the board to Joe.

Joe signed, a little taken aback. How did the doctor suddenly know his name? He never ever used his middle name although it was obviously in his records.

The man in the Land Rover handed him a pass attached to a neck strap.

'Please wear that at all times when in this area.' The man returned to his paperwork and ignored the doctor and Joe.

'Right, Joe, we will go and join the party.'

Joe followed the doctor towards the marquee that had the

security. As they approached, the guard on the entrance held up his hand and indicated that they stop.

'Gentlemen, please identify yourselves.

Joe noticed that the guard's weapon was now pointing at them and that another sentry off to the right was paying them particular attention. The guard passed a scanner over the ID cards; each time he looked at the screen then to Joe's and the doctor's faces.

'You may proceed, gentlemen,' the guard said, sounding rather superior.

Inside the marquee was a long table with place settings all around three edges. The fourth edge had a large monitor suspended about five feet from the floor. At each seat was a set of headphones and a control box with several switches on it. There were also pencils and paper laid out for each participant. It seemed that Joe and the doctor were the first to arrive.

'What's going on here, Jonathan?' By now Joe was a little curious about things; why was he here and what was he expected to add to this obviously august meeting?

'Just the final part of this slice of the action; we will get a good idea of what is to be done in the next twenty minutes or so.' The doctor sat down at one of the side places and indicated that Joe should sit next to him.

Several other people, mainly men but also two women, one of them very tall and blonde, came in, some said hello to the doctor, some didn't; all looked at Joe a little too long for his comfort.

Finally the background chatter ceased as a very large and very overweight man came in with a bunch of files under his arm. He seemed to have a flunky of some sort, a tall skinny man with no hair at all, who stood behind and to the right of him. *Perhaps he has some medical condition*, Joe thought to himself.

'Ladies and gentlemen,' the large man said in a very clear and loud voice; everyone was looking up the table at him. 'For those that do not know me, I am William Bobb of the joint committee that is overseeing this little episode. I, however, know all of you so I will do the introductions.'

Without notes he went round the table introducing everybody and giving a small outline of their credentials. Joe was getting a little squirmy as he came to him.

'Joe Brunt from the Special Task Team – we will refer to as the STT from now on. The STT have not been involved at this level previously but now we know more about the nature of the beast it is thought they may be useful. Joe has been involved with this current object and the previous one in Oman.'

He moved on, introducing the others that were left. Joe looked at the tall blonde woman as her name was announced. 'Nalia Gamosk is the project director of October, the high-orbit observation satellite that has been in constant use and has provided much valuable information.'

'Lily, please,' she said and smiled. *Russian or from Ukraine or somewhere near,* Joe thought, *good English though.*

With the introductions over, Joe was thinking what possible use he would be to this group and how did this bloke, someone he had never met before, know all about him. *I wonder if I am going to get some more money for this.*

'Ladies and gentlemen, as we have several different languages here; you may make use of the audio translation by using the headphones that are in front of you, however, where possible the discussion will be conducted in English. So, before we start the briefing, are there any points that anyone thinks should be raised at the start?'

'Professor Bobb.' A man on the other side of the table to Joe had his hand in the air.

'Yes, Michael.' The big man indicated with his hand that this "Michael" should speak.

Michael, an overweight man in his forties with an unkempt beard and receding hair, cleared his throat and stood up. 'I do not see the requirement to have the military here.' He waved his hand in the direction of Joe. 'I feel it will be counterproductive and may make matters worse as we find out more about the objects and the anomaly. We should not be taking an overtly aggressive stance.'

'We already have, Michael; remember, we have used nuclear weapons and possibly destroyed at least three of the objects. We have already demonstrated that we may not be that friendly. Hopefully the briefing will set your mind at ease and explain the situation in more depth. Besides the STT are not the military.' The STT were in fact a little more useful than conventional military, certainly in any covert or clandestine operation that may need to be carried out. They had been involved in many small operations over the past twenty years but, as far as Joe knew nothing of this nature. Joe did realise that he was only ever told the minimum information that he needed to do the job. It was very rare that he or any of his team would be given the whole picture – what you don't know you cannot talk about. Joe liked it that way; he wasn't concerned about the why and wherefore, he just took the money and did the job.

'Anyone else?' The professor looked around the table; no one else indicated they wished to speak.

Joe was thinking. *Well at least one person doesn't want me here, maybe there are more but they don't want to step up.*

Michael had glanced sideways at Joe as he sat down but blinked first when he saw Joe looking at him. Joe wasn't bothered in the slightest; he saw all these organisations and tasks simply as a job. He got on with some people and didn't with others; none of that mattered. What did matter was the job in hand; concentrate on that, get it done, go home.

'OK, some of you know more of the background to this than do others.' The professor was speaking and at the same time rearranging his notes. 'So I will start from the beginning – at least what we think might have been the beginning – of this little episode.'

'I would like to let Dr Jonathan Smyth have the first go at this explanation; he will fill you all in on some historical background to what we have encountered. Dr Smyth, please.' The professor waved his hand in the doctor's direction.

The doctor stood and for what seemed like an age didn't say anything but simply looked around the table.

'Ladies and gentlemen, you may recall that way back in 1964 through to 1971 NASA carried out the Mariner programme. In all, five vehicles were sent to Mars; it should have been six but one failed on launch. These vehicles provided hundreds of photographs and masses of data from the Red Planet. This information in turn led to the Viking series of missions that enabled the team to put two landers onto the surface of Mars.'

The doctor paused as if thinking about what he was about to say.

'All fine so far; the information we received was fantastic but not wholly unexpected. We were able to analyse the makeup of the Martian atmosphere and get some very good images of the Martian surface.

'After that we had to wait until 1996 and the Mars Pathfinder vehicle; this time we landed the Sojourner Rover and were able to move about on the surface. Again the imagery and data returned was unprecedented. We had put it down on what appeared to be a large ancient flood plain in the Mars Northern Hemisphere known as Ares Vallis.'

The doctor's audience were paying particular attention now; Joe was wondering where all this was going? Martians?

'So up to this point we had spent thirty-two years getting through many billions of US dollars. We had lots of data and many millions of photographs of the surface.'

The doctor nodded to a man standing at the back who switched on the large TV screen at the end of the table.

'Then we found this.'

8.

The screen came on and showed a slightly out of focus image of the Martian surface, strewn with rocks of various sizes. A very hazy horizon could be determined over what seemed a low mountain range. The sky was a pinky-grey colour.

The audience, Joe included, were staring at the screen. 'What are we looking at, professor?' Joe was the first to speak.

'Yes, the team missed it at first but when the imagery was cleaned up it became a little more obvious.' The doctor called up the next image, a clearer version of the first with a wider field of view.

The doctor had everyone's attention now. The picture on the screen showed a small shiny object that was sticking out of the ground; just the top of it could be seen. There was no indication as to how big it was and it was very difficult to determine how far away. Without scale it was just a shiny thing just right of the centre of field.

'I can tell you that the object you are looking at is approximately twenty-two metres away from the Rover and is about the size and shape of a forty-gallon oil drum, it does look smaller but we have measured this image and others many times.'

There were gasps from the assembled group; all realising that they were looking at an object that appeared to be the same as the ones that had been landing around the globe over the last year.

The doctor changed the picture, showing the same object but from a different angle. The pictures continued to change as the Rover had moved and taken more images. They had obviously moved the Rover to get a better look.

'Ladies and gentlemen, these images are not in the public domain and have previously only been seen by a small select group. Obviously this would be world news if it were known that we had found something like this on the surface of Mars. Since the object is nearly buried in the surface we have been able to guess at how long it might have been there, judging by the amount of material that is obscuring it. It lies on the edge of an ancient flood plain and is embedded in some older rock outcrop. Give or take a few million years we reckon it has lain in this position for around half a billion Earth years.'

The doctor was looking around the table trying to gauge the general feeling of the group.

'Has any further investigation been carried out on this object since it was discovered?' Lily was speaking and asking what many of the group were thinking.

'Not much, we drove the Rover around it, photographed it and even prodded it but it seems to be completely inert. No radiation of any sort is being emitted by it. It appears to be dead, if that is the right word to use. None of the subsequent visits to Mars have turned up anything else but considering the size of the area we have been looking that is not surprising.'

'Doctor, I am amazed that we haven't seen these pictures before; they must have caused quite a stir when they first came out of the System.' A middle-aged lady sat next to Joe was speaking. The "System" she was speaking of was a large computer complex at NASA; it had been upgraded over the years and was now very different from the time these images were taken but it was still always referred to as the System.

'The System can be set to exclude almost anything that comes from the outside; it has several protocols to filter and restrict imagery and data. It has a very complex need-to-know setup. Any anomaly is automatically withheld and is flagged to the control group who are the only ones that can access the information. These images and all data concerning the object were withheld and since nothing that came from Mars was "live" it wasn't too difficult to keep a lid on this but you are right in saying they caused quite a stir.' The doctor had finished speaking.

Professor Bobb was on his feet again. 'We thought that we should share this information with you as it may give us a clue as to what purpose these things serve.

'As doctor Smyth has indicated, this particular object arrived on Mars way before man and indeed most life evolved on Earth. We think that, because there have been at least three of these things land on Earth that we know of, there are more here and almost certainly more on Mars.

'Well what should we do about it?' The professor looked around the table; no one spoke.

'A rhetorical question, of course, ladies and gentlemen,' Professor Bobb said almost immediately.

'The object on Mars is not of interest at this time; if we could go there and have a good look at it perhaps it would be useful but since we cannot we must concentrate on the objects that have appeared here on this planet.' The professor was now thinking while he looked through the top few pages of his notes.

'The possible impact the object had on Mars, however, is of interest and I would like you all to stay with me as I set out a scenario.' Professor Bobb put his notes on the table. 'There is some agreement regarding the possible history of the Planet Mars; probably held a reasonable atmosphere and almost certainly large amounts of water in a liquid state. It would have certainly had a greater gravitational field than it does today due in a great part to it having a liquid core.' William Bobb was away in thought for a moment then continued.

'We know that because the gravitational field is so weak, Mars cannot retain a significant density of atmosphere; no atmosphere, no water and very exposed surface results – not a great place to live. In fact, it is concluded that even if life did exist on Mars in the past it certainly does not today.' He paused, gauging his audience.

'Subsequent visits to the Red Planet have found not a trace of life in any form. Again, although we have only looked at a miniscule part of the whole surface, we are confident our findings are typical of the whole.

'Using all the available data and a bit of guesswork we have deduced that this object appeared on Mars prior to the change in the gravitational field and that the object, along with an unknown number of others, somehow modified the molten core of Mars thereby reducing the strength of the gravitational field. The atmosphere slipped away into space and Mars became a barren wilderness that could not support life as we know it. Yes, Ian?' The professor was looking at a middle-aged man a few places down from him; Doctor Ian Munro, Astrophysicist.

'It seems to be a huge jump from a possible, a "could have been", to the result you are suggesting; we find an object on Mars and from that we have deduced that it somehow modified the Martian core to cause the atmosphere to depart and kill the planet. A bit of a jump, if you don't mind me saying.' There were a few nods in agreement around the table.

'Quite right to question this but we are pretty certain this happened in Mars' past because we are also pretty certain it is happening here on Earth – right now.'

There was a sudden outbreak of chatter around the table, most trying to grasp the enormity of what had just been said.

'Ladies and gentlemen, please, we have a lot more to get through before we can start putting a plan into place.'

The noise subsided and everyone's attention was back onto the professor. He nodded to the man controlling the TV screen; a map of the world came up and on it were three red markers, one of them in Wales.

'As you can see these are the three objects that we know of: one over here in Siberia, one in the Empty Quarter of Oman and one here not three miles from where we sit. We believe that it is likely that there are, or will be, many more, but before we move on to what we can do about any of this, please have a look at two images that came back from a spacecraft called Mariner 10 in 1974. We didn't place any importance on them at the time and it was thought they might just be photographic anomalies and not real objects at all. It was only when we were considering the Mars object that we dug through the history of other missions.'

A black and white image came onto the screen; it seemed to be of cloud with an object just on the edge of it. The image appeared to show the cloud and object from above, like many such photographs taken by the many astronauts in space over the last twenty or so years. Joe had seen hundreds online every time the news mentioned the missions that succeeded or failed. The next image came on and was a closer, clearer version of the first: lots of cloud with a cylindrical object just above it. Joe thought it was odd they were showing this; it was obviously one of the cylinders entering the Earth's atmosphere over the last couple of months.

Some of the audience let out a gasp as the professor spoke.

'Some of you will remember the Mariner 10 mission; its aim was to end up looking at Mercury, which it did a very good job of and provided lots of useful information about that planet at the time. However, on its way to Mercury it did a brief flyby of Venus and, from the many images captured, these came back to Earth. We cannot be certain but by judging the object against the curvature of the planet and knowing the distance it was from the camera we think this is another of the objects. How long it has been in orbit and what it is doing is an unknown but we did not detect any radiation from it. The technology available was not what it is today but the spacecraft was looking at the radioactive spectrum as it went past and nothing different from background was detected.

'But that was an aside to the task in hand and I would now like to let Professor Billy Glapton speak.'

A man in his late thirties stood up. *Spends a lot of time playing sport or a lot of time in the gym.* Joe thought, watching the second professor to speak stand up.

'Ladies and gentlemen, I would like to explain the detail behind the conclusions that Professor Bobb has outlined.' Billy Glapton spoke with a natural authority and with a voice that could make money reading audiobooks. *He would be good on TV and radio*, Joe was thinking.

'What many of you are thinking is correct; we could not possibly conclude that the demise of Mars' gravitational field was due to an object that was seen half buried in the surface, however, it does appear to be identical to the ones found on Earth and maybe the one seen in orbit around Venus. Is this a coincidence? Perhaps, but the ones on Earth are not dormant and do appear to serve a purpose; what that purpose is, we are not yet certain.'

The professor stopped and the screen flashed up a picture of the first object that had been found in Siberia. *Looks the same*. Joe thought, not having known of this one before the briefing.

Bill Glapton cleared his throat and carried on. 'This one,' he indicated the picture on screen, 'was throwing out all sorts of radiation at all wavelengths from lower end radio all the way up to gamma and beyond. I say beyond because we lost it as it went past the gamma frequencies and then came back down. All this happened in a series of sweeps, up then down and back again.

'At first we thought that the transmission had ceased at the top and bottom frequencies i.e. turned off then on again, but this wasn't the case. We had placed several monitoring devices close to the object to try and gain an idea of direction and intensity of the emissions. This instrumentation soon led us to believe that the frequency changes did not stop but merely went outside of what we currently know to be the limits. Obviously we all know that the frequency change is theoretically infinite and this seems to provide evidence to support that theory. How far this "sweep" went into the unknown is… unknown.

'Secondly we discovered that there were two distinct types of emissions. One was in bursts that radiated out from the object in all directions including into the ground. These emissions were very high intensity but only lasted less than a second; they were, however, over the whole frequency range – quite remarkable. The second type was in the x-ray to gamma band and at a much lower intensity. This second emission lasted much longer, sometimes as long as half a minute, and seemed to be directed at particular things. For instance when personnel or vehicles approached, the object would emit low level x-ray and move into the gamma frequency momentarily then back to x-ray then stop.'

The gathering remained silent as Bill paused for a sip of

water. Joe was now very interested in what was being said and all sorts of thoughts were going through his head. Who or what was behind all this, and what was it trying to do?

'From this and subsequent encounters we believe that the object is scanning anything close to it to determine threat. Going on from that we believe that this first object did not recognise anything we were doing was any danger it at all.

'As most of you know, we did try all manner of attacks against this object but all failed, with no perceivable damage to it. That is until we tried the Electrical Discharge Weapon that has been under development for some years.'

The professor put up a picture showing the Electrical Discharge Weapon set up and aimed at the object, very similar to the way the one in Oman was done.

'What I will show you now is a short video clip as the weapon was discharged at the object.' A long-range image appeared on the screen showing the object but not the weapon. The picture changed to a close-up view of the object. 'The clip will run in real time, then I will show you a much sloweddown version that I'm sure you will find interesting.'

The screen showed nothing different for a couple of seconds then there was a massive flash of light that exceeded the camera's ability to capture the image. It seemed to last much longer than it actually did, which was just under two seconds. The picture was re-established and showed nothing but an empty area where the object had been: no object, no debris, nothing but open ground.

'Now we have much slowed imagery from about a tenth of the normal speed to a hundredth. See what happens as the object is hit.'

The next clip started with the same view of the object sat on the frozen ground; the wait for anything to happen seemed to go on for ages then the object changed colour; a moment later the electrical discharge could be seen lancing towards it. As contact was made the discharge seemed to penetrate the object then the massive white light started to grow from the screen. Just before the white out of the image, the object seemed to fall apart and spread out with the flash. Then it was gone. The professor showed the clip again; this time, as the discharge reached the object, the clip slowed down to noticeable steps. The object seemed to become transparent then fracture into ever-decreasing sized particles until it was not visible, then white out.

'Let me go back a couple of frames and explain what was happening as the object was hit.'

The image returned to the object with the discharge about to contact it.

'OK, we will hold the sequence there; at this time the object began putting out low level x-ray and gamma as if it was scanning the discharge. As it was hit, the radiation output ceased and at the same time the structure of the object began to change as if it was breaking down into very small parts.'

At this point, the professor had advanced the clip a couple of steps. 'A large burst of radiation all across the spectrum was emitted from the object but this time was directed upwards, slightly off vertical. We only captured the discharge by pure luck because a drone passed over the area at ten thousand feet. It only lasted a millisecond. After that as you saw the object seemed to evaporate leaving no trace and, believe me, we did look at the area down to the microscopic.'

The overweight Michael was waving his hand in the air. 'Yes, Michael.'

'Excuse me, professor, but why, at this early stage, were we being so aggressive?'

'Remember the high-intensity burst of radiation right across the spectrum? Well it seems that it was not just a burst of energy for the sake of it; it was directed and was doing something.'

The professor looked across at Lily who had been leafing through some notes that she had in front of her. 'I think that our colleague, Lily, can be of help here.' The professor sat down.

'Ladies and gentlemen, I am Lily, Director of the October high-Earth-orbit project. As you may know the October facility is in high orbit around the Earth, just outside the orbit of the Moon. It was recently used in the identification of the anomaly that so tragically caused the death of two Russian cosmonauts. Whether this was by design or coincidental we do not know but they were lost.' She waited to indicate that the loss of the two cosmonauts was important to her.

'Before and after this event we have been monitoring the Earth's magnetic field; it was part of a long-term study of the effect of solar flare activity and how this affected Earth. Most of the data collected was not outside of what we already knew or expected. Then the object that landed in Siberia made us pay a little more attention. We soon detected the high-yield radiation that it was transmitting but couldn't at first determine what it was for because it was all across the spectrum. After a few days, however, a ground station in the Ural Mountains contacted the project to ask if we too were noticing anything odd or unexpected with regards to the current state of the Earth's magnetic field; there had been no solar flare activity so we did not think that we would find anything out of the ordinary, but we did.'

Lily put up a graph onto the screen and used a laser pointer to highlight areas of interest for the audience. 'At this point,' she pointed at the left or start of the graph, 'we have normal measurements of the field that radiates from the Earth.' The graph was flat, except for a couple of blips, about halfway across; each section represented a week so the point she was indicating was about three weeks from the start of the record. 'Then this.' She indicated a very steep up-and-down wave that lasted, according to the graph, about half a day then a flat line again with the normal blips.

'This large rise and decrease coincides with the radiation bursts from the object in Siberia.

'This is the day after the first graph ended.' She had put up a graph that seemed to be the same except that once the line movement had started it continued to oscillate up and down with a short space in between. At each rise in activity of the magnetic field, the object was transmitting. When it stopped the line returned to normal or almost normal. We detected an almost imperceptible decrease in the strength of the Earth's magnetic field. We concluded at this point that it was likely that the transmissions from the object were affecting the field. Greater minds than mine then decided to act.'

Lily sat down and looked up the table at Professor Bobb. *Do I detect a little bit of disagreement here?* thought Joe.

Professor Bobb was on his feet. 'Indeed, it was concluded that we did not know for sure what this thing was doing but we wanted it to stop. We tried the gentle approach and moved on up the scale to a nuclear weapon, albeit a small one. All had no effect that we could determine, so, as a last attempt to change what it was doing, we used the Electrical Discharge Weapon. This made the object stop transmitting and indeed made it go away, or was it destroyed? We don't know.'

'So you can see, ladies and gentlemen, we have, at this point, embarked on a journey from which there is no going back.' The professor called up another image.

'I was on the ground for this one, as were several of you who are here.'

The professor let the audience look at the image before

explaining what was happening. 'The object here appears to be the twin of the one in Siberia but this time it is in the border between Saudi Arabia and the Sultanate of Oman: an area known as the Empty Quarter.'

He called up a similar graph to the one that Lily had previously used. 'This is from the same source as the one Lily was showing you and we are indeed indebted to her project for letting us have this information, without it we would still be somewhat in the dark.

'As you can see the graph follows a similar pattern as the first but this time it is synchronised with the output from the second object, however, the effect on the magnetic field is very slightly greater than the first.'

The professor then explained what had transpired out in the Omani desert; how they had decided to use the Electrical Discharge Weapon first and not try anything else. The result had been the same; the object had disappeared, without trace. Slow motion imagery was a complete rerun of the first. The object had simply evaporated and left no detectable trace on the ground.

'That now leads us to Wales.' The professor looked down the table and indicated a man sat right at the end should speak. 'Doctor Oliver Glapton.' The professor sat down.

'Hello, everybody, I am currently leading the effort here in sunny Wales and if you are thinking I share the same surname with Billy then you have noticed that we are brothers but I am the smart one.'

A smile came to Bill Clapton's face.

'The object appeared here a couple of days ago but it wasn't until today that we knew exactly where it was. It sits in the valley not far from where we are now. This one is different; it doesn't emit radiation in the visible spectrum at all and is not emitting the high-energy discharges that the previous two did.

It is using the x-ray and gamma quite a bit though. So what is it doing? We think that it is hiding from us because we can now destroy it with the Electrical Discharge Weapon, an EDW. How the weapon is successful and a nuclear device is not is not understood. So a couple of things may be happening; perhaps the object is defective and unable to transmit high levels of radiation or…' Oliver paused. '… It is waiting.'

'Waiting for what?' Michael was speaking again. *He likes to ask questions,* Joe thought.

'We really don't know and if it is waiting, we don't know how long it will wait. The main difference with this particular object is that it seemed to defend itself when one of the STT came close to it with an EDW. The man disappeared and only left some of his clothing and the weapon lying on the floor. We conclude that the object, or objects, can now perceive threat.

'Now we have all been brought up to date, what is to be done about this and any other objects that might appear?'

'How do we track these things? How do we know they are even there?' Michael was speaking again.

'We have had varying levels of success so far; the one in Siberia just appeared because we weren't looking for it at the time. The one in Oman was tracked as it entered the atmosphere so it was easy to locate on the ground. This one here was also tracked to this general area but as we now know it is not detectable in the visible spectrum.' Oliver paused as if he was about to say something very important. 'That leaves us with the one that destroyed the soviet vehicle in orbit; we have no idea where that one went but we do have some footage of it as it emerged from the anomaly and collided with the Russian re-supply vehicle. It was the first and is, as far as we can tell, the same as the subsequent two. So with the one here in Wales, that makes four in all, unless we have been missing these things on a regular basis. We do not know what number one is doing or even that it survived entry into the atmosphere. Two and three seemed to be doing the same thing i.e. emitting high-level bursts of radiation. Number four, the one here, is different; we can't see it and it is not, so far, emitting any high-level radiation.'

It was watching. One rotation to start.

'The important thing here is that we seem to have a weapon that can defeat them or at least stop them doing whatever they are doing. An EDW is available here but we have kept it some distance from this object so as not to present an obvious threat. The trick will be getting it within range and using it quickly.' Oliver Glapton winked at his brother as he sat down.

'Thank you, Oliver.' Professor Bobb was on his feet again. 'We now have a decision to make: do we move the EDW into place and use it or do we wait? I am open to suggestions.'

'Professor.' Billy Glapton was on his feet.

'Yes, Bill, let us have your thoughts.'

Billy Glapton spoke clearly and loudly so as to emphasise the importance of what he was saying. 'As I see it we have two choices, both of which may be the wrong one. We can bring in the EDW and fire it at the object, now we know for sure where it is, or we could sit and wait to see what the object will do next. The first option may fail; it could trigger a response from the object, like it did previously down in the valley, or it could work and make the thing go away. If we sit and wait we have no idea what we are waiting for and for how long, however, this may be the safest option because nothing may happen. As for the moment, the object is not radiating any high-level radiation of the type that we have encountered before. I'm of the opinion that perhaps we should not wait. We should have the EDW ready for a quick deployment.' He sat down.

Michael stood up and waved his arm in the air. 'We cannot assume that this thing is a threat until we have evidence to support that; by taking action, as we did in the previous two, we may be going down a road from which there is no return. We know the EDW works so let us wait to see if there is a need for action.'

Lily stood up to speak and all eyes were on her. 'So far we have deduced that these objects are a technology that is beyond anything produced here on Earth; we think that they are not here to see the scenery and, at times, they seem to be completely unaware of us. It is fortunate that we have chanced upon a weapon that can be used against them. I feel we must act against these objects wherever and whenever we find them; perhaps there are more coming all the time, perhaps there are more than enough here to complete whatever plan is in place. Destroy this one now before we are unable to act.'

The discussion moved around the table, going from instant action to doing nothing; the argument became polarised with a simple go-now-or-wait argument.

'OK, everyone, let us remember we are a group that is to advise the grown-ups what course of action they should take. We can advise what we like but we must ensure that we give clear and unambiguous advice that can be actioned. The more vague we are, the more likely that we will be ignored. Let us take a vote on two proposals that I will outline.' William Bobb held his hands up for quiet.

'Option one: we advise that the EDW is deployed without delay and used against the object. Option two: we advise caution and to wait for two days to see if anything is radiated from the object. After this period or if anything happens during this wait period we re-evaluate.'

'With a show of hands, who favours option one?' Several hands went up, Billy and Oliver being two of those in favour. The professor counted and made a note on his scribble pad.

'Option two?' Again hands were in the air one of them belonging to Michael who liked to ask questions.

Joe had voted for option one, as did Lily, but Joe had no real conviction that either option was going to be the answer. The professor scribbled down the result.

'We have an even split, ladies and gentlemen, so it looks like I have the casting vote.

'We will recommend that option one be implemented as soon as is practicable; let me remind you all that this is only the recommendation from this committee and may or may not be acted upon by the governmental group that is in control.'

The professor looked tired, Joe thought, as the chatter returned.

'It will take time to formally record our decision and present it; can I assure you all that both options will be set out with our recommendation that option one is used. I repeat that this does not determine what the governmental group will decide to do.'

The meeting began breaking up; some left immediately, others stood around and continued the discussion. Jonathan came over to Joe and ushered him away from the group. 'We want you, Joe, to select a couple of men from your team and prepare to be deployed elsewhere.'

9.

Joe was taken by surprise at this. 'What am I expected to do and where am I going?'

'Just get the team ready and let me know when you are in a position to move. The helicopter over there is for you,' he pointed to a Blackhawk that was parked on the edge of the area. 'I would think that you and two others will be enough. You will be taking the Glapton brothers with you – don't worry, they are quite capable in the physical world.' Joe had started to protest but gave up. 'Meet up here in about six hours.' The doctor said as he walked off.

Joe stared over at the chopper; it would be a team of five then so plenty of room in the aircraft but what to take and how long would they be away? He reverted back to Standard Operating Procedures (SOP) and guessed. Once in the control tent he gave orders to the operator who was sat at the communications desk. 'Get a hold of Tom Jones; ask him to come over here and ask him to bring Derek Stevenson with him.' Tom's family name wasn't Jones of course but like many nicknames used in this profession "Jones" had stuck, so Tom Powell was known as Tom Jones by everybody.

The setup here was probably going to have most of what he and his team required but Joe was going to check while he still had the time; weapons, clothing and communication would be essential, food maybe, depending on how long they wanted him for and how far they were going.

Having organised the required kit at the stores he wandered over to see if anything else was happening in control; very quiet with no new action from the valley since he and the doctor had been down there.

'Where do you think we are going, Joe?' The two Glapton brothers seemed to have appeared from nowhere. Billy Glapton was speaking, his brother next to him, both holding Joe's stare.

'Don't know, mate, but I'm sure someone will tell us any time now.' The two brothers certainly looked the part and would have blended in with any of Joe's team. *Are they as good as they look?* Joe mused. It had turned out that Billy Glapton and his brother, Oliver, had spent time in the military and were both Royal Marine Reservists. *These two seem to be able to jam an awful lot of hours into the day!* Joe had thought when he read the brief that had been thrust into his hand.

Just then Tom and Derek came jogging over. 'What's up, boss? Tom said, putting a small bag onto the ground.

'Don't know yet but we are to be deployed elsewhere with these two gentlemen. Tom, Derek, meet Billy and Oliver Glapton – yep, they are brothers. All four shook hands. But none of the men said anything. All were now curious as to what they would all be doing in a couple of minutes: a more serious episode seemed to be unfolding.

Joe addressed the four men. 'I have organised the kit we will need to take along but as I don't fully understand what we will be doing I have got most of the general inventory that we usually take.

'Arms?' Tom asked the question.

'Yes, Glock 17 each, and a long arm – an M4A1 – with one M870 shotgun in the team. As much ammo as we can manage.

We may have to take an EDW but we will have to wait and see about that requirement.'

All five started to assemble and adjust the equipment that had been brought over from the stores for them, each taking time to assess whether the kit would sit well and not cause more problems than it solved. They may have to carry this stuff some distance, so better be prepared. Once complete the two civilians did not stand out as anything other than what they were; part of a team that was well used to this sort of thing.

Jonathan was back but this time he was carrying a black briefcase. 'Joe, walk with me and I'll fill you in on what we want your team to do.' He turned and waited for Joe to appear by his side. 'Over there, I think, will be good.' Jonathan walked towards a small tent that sat next to the big marquee.

Once inside the two men sat either side of a wooden table facing each other. 'Joe, we need you to go here and have a look at something that has been discovered.' Jonathan had laid a large-scale map on the table. Joe didn't immediately recognise the location but it showed an area with steep terrain and a fair amount of water in the valley bottoms.

'Where is it and why aren't we waiting for the committee recommendations to be put to the government group?'

The doctor smiled. 'We are moving in more than one direction from here, the committee's recommendations will be put to the Government group but we cannot wait for that to happen, bearing in mind that any recommendations given will have to be discussed and a conclusion reached. Don't worry about what the government group will or will not decide, your job is clear and will proceed as soon as possible. Now let us talk about what we want you and your team to do.'

The doctor pointed to a spot on the map. 'This point here is in the Republic of Ireland, over on the west coast. It is sparsely populated so you should not encounter any locals; if you do, you are to avoid direct contact. ' Jonathon was smiling again. 'Of course you are not actually there so denial will be the first response from us. Happy with that?' Joe had been here before in a dozen similar situations of course. *We sent you there but we do not know anything about you being there – excellent!'*

'Yes, happy with that,' Joe said now becoming interested in the map; he had been looking at it as the doctor was speaking. *'Same old, same old.'*

'Just to remind you, this is secret so nothing should be written or recorded; all notes to remain in your head; the map is not special but should not be marked up.' The doctor was merely reminding Joe of the normal rules for things like this.

'This is where you will drop off.' The doctor was indicating a track that had come up the side of the hill from the valley floor.

The gradient coming up was quite steep but levelled out as it neared the crest of the ridge. *Looks like a good place for the chopper to get in then out again – quite hidden at this point from the local area.* Joe thought.

'You will insert at 00:30 hours tomorrow and move to the contact point to get a sight of what is there.' The doctor's finger was moving over the map. 'Once in this area you will wait and report back to me that you are ready for the next phase. At this time you and your team are not to cross the ridgeline here; stay south of it until directed otherwise.'

Joe was thinking that this was more vague than it needed to be but he kept quiet and listened, making mental notes regarding the local area as he went. It seemed that the area was not populated, with the nearest buildings being about eight miles away to the south, certainly nothing in the area in which he was to operate.

'The point of interest is here.' The doctor indicated a gully system that was over the ridge and down in the adjoining valley. 'Down here is a cave system that extends back into the hill for around two hundred metres. The system has been explored in the past but it is too far off the beaten track to be of any interest to tourists and the like; there is enough headroom to enable the average man to stand but the roof comes down to about two feet or so as you get near to the deepest point. It then stops so there are no wriggle holes or the like to contend with.' The cave's extent was marked out with a dotted line faintly on the map. 'The cave outline on this map is not one hundred per cent accurate so bear that in mind.

'When we give your team the nod we would like you to enter the cave system and determine what, if anything is there. Any questions so far?' The doctor was looking at Joe, raising an eyebrow.

'So we are to be inserted here to wait for the go; then we move over the ridge and go down to the valley floor and enter the caves. Then what? And what should we expect? Are there any watercourses or steep climbs or drops in the system? Are we free or tight?' Joe was referring to the weapon state and permissions he should be following.

'Weapons-free from when you get off the chopper. However, if you encounter anything that you think your team should shoot at then please do so – you have absolute authority in this area. At this time of year there are no active watercourses within the cave system and there are no climbs or drops that require special equipment.' The doctor was now reading some notes he had on the table.

'Oh, and Joe, we don't think that the small arms you will no doubt take will pose any threat to these things but they may be useful to deter close scrutiny from any local gendarmerie that might show up.'

'Now the background info that requires you to go there and have a look.' Jonathan placed a large piece of paper onto the table. 'This is the list of events from this location so far. As you can see, detailed here are transmissions from this point over a period of ten weeks ending yesterday.' The doctor was tracing his finger down the page. 'Each entry here was recorded as a transmission of, what we think, are X-rays but it could be something else. The X-ray detector picked it up anyway.' The doctor produced another piece of paper, on which was a similar list of events. 'You may have noticed that both these lists seem to be identical in timescale. What we think is happening is every time the object in Wales transmits, something in this part of Ireland does the same. We did an awful lot of tracking and have come to the conclusion that the something that is responding to the object is in these caves; if not in the caves than very close by.'

'What do you want me to do with what we find in the cave, Jonathan?' Joe was looking for clarification; it seemed to him that he was being given a completely free hand in this.

'If you can, destroy it; destroy all and everything you find. If you cannot do that, run away.'

'You will need to get your men briefed and be on the chopper within an hour; we want you to be on time, give or take ten minutes or so. Once you are on the aircraft, complete radio silence until you are on the ridge ready to go. The flight crew have been briefed so no need to discuss any of this with them. They will drop you off just over the ridgeline and will then leave you to it; extraction will be on your request. Only take the Pinger with you.' The Pinger was a modern version of the old pager that many people used to use. The Pinger would work in both directions via satellite with a transmission time of less than a tenth of a second. They were particularly difficult for listeners to pinpoint.

'And Joe!' One last word from the doctor. 'Take the EDW with you; it has been modified to increase output somewhat.'

Joe used the time to go back to the stores and pick up some X19 demolition charges; these had proven invaluable on previous outings when items of equipment needed disabling. *Disabling?* Joe thought that completely destroyed would be a better turn of phrase. He collected the EDW on the way out.

'I wonder if the cave thing will perceive us as a threat carrying this thing,' Joe said to himself as he walked back to the four men who were now sat on the ground near the chopper. All seemed to be very relaxed and had been talking, introducing themselves to each other, comparing past experiences.

'For a bunch of civvies you all look the part at least,' Joe said, not expecting an answer. He didn't get one.

'Right oh, get where you can see the map and we will go over what we are expected to do.' Joe laid the map on the floor so they could all see. 'Not too much to take in gentlemen; we are going to be dropped off here and wait. Once told to move, we will move over the ridgeline and make our way into the valley. Down here,' Joe indicated with a finger, 'is a network of caves; somewhere in these caves, or close by, is our target.'

'What do we expect to find boss?' Derek was speaking.

'We don't know but when we find it we will do our best to destroy it. This is not a touchy feely mission; we have only one aim: total destruction.' Joe thought that he sounded a bit too ambitious but hey, other people were calling the shots. That was the only question; perhaps it had answered everything the others wanted to know. The Glapton brothers seemed content with the plan but said nothing. He had worked with Tom on many occasions, eyes and ears open, mouth shut kind of man.

The Blackhawk lifted off and flew west into the night; it would be a couple of hours at least until they were in the area to be put down. Joe had lost count of the times he had been sat in the back of some helicopter or another over the last couple of years; he had been doing this for most of his working life. Although he was no longer in the military he was still a soldier of sorts, being used when conventional forces could not be. He looked out into the darkness and noted that they were still very low; the wave tops could clearly be seen. *We're hiding*, he thought to himself.

Joe was watching the two Glapton brothers who were next to each other on the other side of the helicopter; they were both asleep or appeared to be asleep. *I wonder if they know a little more than I do*. Joe wasn't bothered if they did; he knew what he was supposed to do: get in, destroy the target, leave – elementary.

He went over the detail from the map that he had committed to memory; no local farms or houses within a couple of miles of the target; no main routes in the area and only a single farm track that had not been in use when last surveyed. Quite a wild part of Ireland. Joe wondered if the Irish government knew of their impending arrival – probably not judging by the way the helicopter was being flown – they would cross the coast anytime now, then would fly across land avoiding town and villages where possible. They would be too low to give themselves away to any airport radar. He looked forward to the two pilots, dimly illuminated by the lights from their instruments. Both men were wearing the latest thermal-imaging goggles so they could probably see the terrain quite well; they also had a moving-map device that had been clipped to the instrument panel. Joe hadn't seen one like it before but it seemed to be working; he noted that it showed they had just crossed the coast.

Tom and Derek were talking into each other's ear; the noise, although not deafening, was too loud to let them hold a normal conversation. These two had also been on many operations like this and had not known the full story; they both thought that they were paid sufficiently well to keep the questions to what was required by the job. Minor detail was just that, minor detail. Joe didn't know what they were talking about but if he had to guess they would be talking about equipment and the best use of it. Derek, as well as his Glock 7 and M4A1 assault rifle, had the EDW lying at his feet. *I wonder if we will need that.* Joe was planning for eventualities as usual; a habit he had gotten into in a former life. Always consider what might happen and then some. Don't get surprised by anything that should have been considered but wasn't.

10.

The co-pilot was looking round at Joe; he indicated with his fingers that they were one hour out. Joe acknowledged with a thumbs-up. The co-pilot said something to the pilot over the intercom as he turned round. 'Those two probably know even less than me.' Joe looked out of the window trying to gauge how high they were; he got a glimpse of the odd light as they flew over but not a lot of detail. The helicopter suddenly banked to the right then levelled out again. *Probably avoiding built-up areas,* Joe mused as he closed his eyes and brought up the map in his head again.

The helicopter was banking again; this time to the left and was not straightening up. 'I think we are there,' Joe said out loud, although no one heard him over the engine noise. The thud, thud from the rotors changed as the pitch was altered to give more lift as the aircraft slowed to a standstill. Moments later the helicopter was on the ground. Everyone was in action at the same time; all the kit went out first followed by each man and his personal items. The helicopter was empty within less than a minute. Joe was not surprised by this, but the two Glapton brothers were now behaving like seasoned members of the team; this didn't go unnoticed by the three professionals.

The chopper lifted off and headed west out over the Atlantic Ocean. 'There must be a carrier or some type of support vessel out there,' Joe said to Tom who was also looking at the departing helicopter. 'Hopefully close enough when we shout for extraction.'

They had been dropped off in exactly the right spot, just short of the ridgeline facing North West; it would be a simple hike to get over the crest, move down into the valley on the other side and be in contact with the cave complex.

'OK, everybody, let us get our kit sorted and prepare to move when ordered; I will ping to say we are here but I suspect the chopper has already done that for us.' Joe pressed the transmit button on the device attached to his arm; a faint light blinked to indicate it was functioning correctly. 'Now we will wait and see what the morning brings us.'

At least it wasn't raining and the air temperature was quite warm for this time of year. 'What's your story then?' Joe was addressing Oliver Glapton who was checking his weapon for the tenth time since they had landed. 'I am a theoretical linguist; it was thought that I could be of use if we encountered anything that wanted to talk to us.'

'A theoretical linguist? What is that when it's at home?' Joe said.

Oliver explained that, obviously a linguist was a person dealing with different languages, however, he was not particularly interested in any language but was expert in the way languages were constructed and was very familiar with the rules that governed communication between entities, such as man, that used it. 'We have done a lot of work over the last couple of years in the search for intelligent mechanisms that might be encountered. We do believe that we have now encountered such a beast so here I am.'

'What about you then, Bill? Are you a language man too?' Tom asked, becoming quite interested.

"No, I am a theoretical physicist; I am interested in

how these objects communicate – that's if they are indeed communicating.'

'A physicist and a linguist, in theory,' Joe smiled.

The Pinger bleeped once; Joe looked at the display and looked up. 'We have an hour before we move, that will bring us up to just before first light so the sun will be behind us as we go down the ridge, the bottom of the valley should still be in shade when we reach the cave area.'

'So, Oliver, are we going to try and talk to this thing once we discover what and where it is?' Joe was a little puzzled by the revelation that Oliver did things with communicating.

'No, Joe; the Glaptons are here to assist the team in the destruction of whatever we find; the time for talking has long since passed: we must destroy it. Billy has an idea of how it is communicating and I have an idea of what it is saying but our previous work will not get in the way of the task in hand; we are part of this team that was sent for one purpose only. I promise you we will not get distracted.'

Joe was on his feet. 'Gentlemen, we have about twenty minutes to go, so we should remind ourselves on the plan.' He put the map onto the ground as he knelt down; he didn't think for one minute that Tom and Derek needed to see it again; like him they would have it stored firmly in their heads. He noted that neither Billy nor Oliver paid too much attention to it either; they were getting better all the time, he thought. He was inclined to pump the Glaptons for more information but that could wait; the task now was clear and about to start: no distractions at this time.

'We will break into two groups; Billy, you come with me and, Oliver, you go with Tom; Derek I want you to follow my group down the hill but keep about a hundred metres behind us; we know that the EDW has some sort of effect on the way these things have acted in the past so we will keep you out of the way as backup. Team one, that's me and Billy, will enter the valley at this point and move down in a south-westerly direction following this.' Joe was tapping the map, indicating a narrow gully that went into the valley. 'Team two will move down to the other end of this feature and descend down via this track.' There was a small track indicated on the map that seemed to end just before the bottom of the valley and about fifty metres from the entrance to the cave system. 'I know there isn't much detail on this map but I am assured that the contour profile is one hundred per cent accurate, so no big holes or drops to take us by surprise. Any questions before we move to the ridgeline?' Joe was looking at each in turn; there were no questions. 'Right then, get your kit on and move to the start points; team one has the furthest to go so team two will leave five minutes after.'

The five men made final adjustments to the equipment they were carrying and then split into three and moved to the start point; the dawn was just starting to show as the gloom receded.

'Good luck, everybody,' Tom said to no one in particular as he watched Joe and the other two move over the ridge and disappear down into the valley. Five minutes later he and Oliver moved off, crested the ridge and moved down the valley side until they crossed the track that had been indicated on the map. *Map's good so far,* Tom thought. Oliver was following behind at the standard distance; not to be too close to catch the same incoming as Tom but not too far away to be unable to render assistance should it be needed.

'What are they doing?' The second watcher commented.

'I do not know but they may have to be removed if they come too close; the start is approaching and they cannot be allowed to delay it.' The two watched all five men moving down the valley towards them.

'There is a weapon with the last one,' the second watcher said. 'Why is it not with the others?'

Oliver was looking at a small box that he had removed from the small satchel he was carrying. 'We are being watched,' he said just loud enough for Tom to hear.

'Watched? How do you know that?' Tom was more than a little surprised at this information.

'A little bit of kit I built for this eventuality. Not that clever but when we came over the ridgeline the traffic picked up and is now almost constant. Conclusion? If they are talking about us they are watching us. It would appear that they did not notice our presence when we landed behind the ridge, I would have thought that they would have clocked the chopper as we came in. Interesting don't you think?'

Tom was looking down the valley to where Joe and team one were making progress. 'Does your brother have one of those?' he asked.

'Of course.' Oliver replied, sounding like the question was completely unnecessary. 'I have another little piece of equipment that we should now deploy.' Oliver removed another small box from the same satchel.

'What is that?' Tom was beginning to think he was watching a "rabbit out of the hat" type show. Oliver was holding a small rectangular box with several switches and dials on it.

'We discovered that they are confused by counter transmissions using the same wavelength as they transmit. It doesn't appear that the output is at all relevant; they blast it out and we return it, even at very low output and they get confused. Neat, don't you think? As I said, Billy has the same stuff as me so I would presume they are at the same point as we are.'

'And that point is?' Tom was beginning to feel like a passenger in this operation.

'Time to initiate counter measures Tom.' Oliver flicked a switch and two of the dials lit up: one showing the needle into the red and the other showing into the green. Oliver adjusted the device so that both dials showed the pointer in the green. 'All set!' Oliver smiled as he put the device back into the satchel.

Tom sat down and took out a small pair of binoculars, adjusting them for the low light and looked in the direction of team one further along the valley. He saw that they too were stopped and were talking; Derek remained about a hundred metres or so up the side of the re-entrant. 'They seem to be having the same conversation as we have just had.'

He watched Joe turn and look in their direction; waiting for a moment then lifting his arm in the signal to proceed.

'They have gone!' One of the two watchers was taken by surprise, as the group of five seemed to disappear from the side of the valley.

'It is of no concern; we are not able to determine where they have gone or even if they ever existed. It does not affect the outcome; we should prepare to return the individual.'

The five men made good progress and reached the valley floor as the sun came up; the steepness of the valley wall meant they were still in shadow and would be for some time yet.

Both teams were now about one hundred metres from the entrance to the cave system but on opposite sides; Derek was still holding back away from the other two members of his group. Both teams could see each other a little more clearly now as the light level increased as the dawn was breaking across the whole of the landscape. It looked like it was to be a fine day.

All four men now began a sweep of the route to the cave entrance with Derek keeping over watch from his position up the side of the valley. They moved carefully checking for recent activity or anything that would indicate that anyone had been this way in recent days; they found nothing, no marks are any surface damage in the surrounding area. They met in front of the cave system entrance; Tom was the first to speak. 'Nothing so far.' He was addressing Joe who was busy with the Pinger on his arm.

'No, I have told them we are here and ready to proceed; so we should make ourselves as comfortable as we can here for now,' Joe said.

The two teams were now waiting for instructions; they made the best of the time by dropping some of the equipment they had been carrying – normal routine for operations in confined spaces – so there was less to get in the way should they need to move quickly.

'What about Derek?' Tom was thinking that perhaps Derek should be with any part of the team that entered the cave.

'Yes, I see what you are saying, it might be useful if we had the weapon with us; all angles covered.' Joe waved at Derek and gave the signal to close with the group.

Now all five members were together, Joe set out the plan to be followed. He, Derek and Oliver would enter the cave system when they had the go-ahead from control. Tom and Billy would remain outside and act as a reserve should one be needed. It shouldn't take more than forty minutes to search the caves if the information they had regarding the complexity of the system was correct. Joe decided that they would not go into any area that was below five feet. Once the plan had been outlined they all checked and rechecked the equipment they carried.

'How long have we had the jammer, Oliver?' Tom was stood looking at Oliver who had just been adjusting the device on his arm.

'A year or so; we spent some considerable time trying to

figure out how they were communicating but we think that we now know. After that it was fairly easy to come up with the jammer.' Oliver paused as if he was thinking about if he should say more about the device. 'Billy and I determined that they, whoever or whatever "they" are, have been using short bursts of radiation at varying wavelengths to modify the atmosphere around them. This is in addition to the massive transmissions that appear to be affecting the Earth's gravitational field. We haven't the faintest idea how it all works but we soon found that if we transmit on a random frequency at very low output the bad guys – if they are indeed bad – get confused; usually the transmissions from them decrease then stop all together.'

'So the emissions from the cave have now stopped,' Tom said.

'Yes, not a squeak since I switched this on.' Oliver tapped the device. 'So unless they have switched to another method of scanning then I think they are unaware that we are so close. Of course, they may have many tried and tested ways of doing things but we think not; previously when we did this there was no activity from them at all as long as the device was turned on.'

'Don't sound too smug, Oliver, we have only scratched the surface of what they are doing. We wouldn't bet money on the chances we have completely stopped them looking at us; it could be the transmissions aren't anything to do with us at all but are random in nature or they weren't even looking at us.' Billy was looking at his own device, which had a small light that was flashing about once a second. 'There is nothing coming out of the cave area now so we can assume they have stopped whatever they were doing.'

Daylight had arrived and was shining very brightly across the valley; the weather was good. There were some dark clouds over to the west but nothing much that would threaten rain anytime soon. The Pinger on Joe's arm beeped once.

11.

'We are good for the next stage.' Joe was sending an acknowledgement back through the system. 'No change in what we are to do: destroy anything that we find in the cave area, no exceptions. Are we all clear on this?' Joe looked at each of them in turn.

'What if we find friendlies or the like in there?' Tom wasn't overly convinced that they should be making this blanket decision before they knew what, if anything, they would be facing.

'Tom, you and I have been in similar positions before; obviously this may turn into something that has more to it but at the moment we are here to do what has been ordered and not much else.' Joe wasn't looking at ether Tom or Derek but held the gaze of Billy and Oliver.

'Tom, I want you and Billy to place two or three demolition charges about twenty feet into the cave entrance; set them to detonate on command from your position outside – we may need to end this little episode quickly should things go pear-shaped.' Joe didn't actually think that events would require the charges but he was just making sure. 'Always have a plan B.'

'OK, let's go,' Joe said as he turned and headed into the cave entrance, switching on his head torch as he strode forward. Joe stayed on point whilst Derek was second with Oliver as last man. Each was separated from the other by around ten feet; close enough to support each other but far enough apart not to get in a single blast of anything. The head torches they were using provided a surprising amount of light; they were able to see easily enough as their eyes became accustomed to the reduced light as they entered the cave.

The object in the Welsh valley was nearing the end of the wait period; it had received no new instructions so at the end of this rotation it would begin. It had been observing the activity a short distance from it; they had put one of the devices in place but it had not been powered. No threat at this time. None of them were near the device. It is now too late for them.

As the team moved into the cave Tom and Billy began assembling and fitting the charges that would be used if it all went belly up. They also made ready the fuel/air weapon that came with the demolition charges. Plan was to fire the weapon into the cave about half a second before detonation of the demolition charges. Tom particularly liked these fuel/air things; they had been around for years in one form or another but this one was particularly handy as it was small enough to carry around. It consisted of a small booster rocket that would enable the warhead to be fired into an object or building – in this case, the cave. Once the warhead detonated, the fuel contained within it would be turned into a rapidly expanding cloud of gas. Then a second detonation would ignite the gas and – boom – mega shockwave, enough to bring down a block of flats. Coupled with the closing cave entrance the pressure inside the cave would be driven up to levels that could not be survived in an instant. Tom was very aware that if anything in the cave was similar in construction to the object in the valley in Wales then this was all a little pointless.

The three men had moved about a hundred metres into the cave when Joe called a halt.

'Very odd already,' Joe said as if he was expecting the odd but not at this time.

'We should be at a turn in the cave system by now.' Joe was aiming his head torch into the darkness in front of them; nothing but the cave walls and darkness was apparent; the cave seemed to go on for some distance in a straight line.

'Oh well, we were told the map was a bit vague at best so perhaps the original survey that has been used to produce the cave outline on the map was at fault; no turn in the cave system but a straight line to the back, about halfway in now.'

They started to move forward again. Joe had slowed the pace down a little, not quite sure about what they might encounter; perhaps nothing but an empty cave system, radiation transmissions or not.

The earth under their feet seemed to pulse, almost imperceptibly, but still suggesting a definite movement or short vibration.

'Did you feel that?' Joe asked the other two. Both were looking at him, their expressions indicated that they had indeed felt something.

'Very short and small rise in radiation in the gamma.' Oliver was looking at the device attached to his arm. 'Nothing like the readings we have encountered so far; only lasted about a tenth of a second – looks like we might have attracted some attention.'

Joe was standing with a hand on the wall of the cave with his head down as if listening. 'Come over here and put your hand on the wall.'

The two men moved and did as they were bid. 'Did you feel that?' Oliver was speaking, looking at the other two in turn; he could tell by their expressions that they had indeed felt something on or inside the wall of the cave. A shimmering vibration that seemed to fade then return; very faint but definitely there.

'What do you think it is? It seems a bit like machinery some distance away but putting vibration into the rock, like a generator or something similar. Doesn't explain the fading though.' Derek now had his head touching the wall to try and get a better feel for the noise.

'OK, we can mention this in our after action report.' Joe made to continue into the cave system.

What happened next took them all by surprise; the vibration was no longer slight but overpowering. The whole cave system seemed to be in convulsions; the cave walls appeared to ripple in time with the vibration but no debris was falling from the roof or anywhere else. All three were on their knees holding their heads to try and block out the sensation. Derek was throwing up and the other two were close to it. All of a sudden the vibration ceased, completely gone. Joe got to his feet and leaned on the cave wall.

'The vibration has gone, at least as far as I can tell,' Joe said, rubbing his eyes his other hand on the wall.

'What was that?' Derek was getting to his feet but looked extremely ill and very unsteady. Oliver was sitting on the ground, looking very unwell.

'Well there was no increase in any radiation so what we felt wasn't noise either. If I had to guess I would say a strong magnetic field had been generated.' Oliver was checking the instrument on his arm, which was telling him that in fact nothing had happened. 'Although it didn't seem to affect any of the metal items we are carrying – most odd.'

They were now all stood together facing the direction of travel. Joe waved his arm indicating they should proceed. After about fifty metres Joe stopped.

'Can you two see that?' Joe was pointing down the tunnel; in the distance was a faint glow that seemed to be round in shape.

'Yep, we see it,' Derek answered for Oliver who was again looking at the instrument on his arm.

'No increase in radiation.' Oliver said after about a minute.

'Right oh, let's be aware and go and see what it is. The cave system doesn't have any other entrances than the one we used to get here so heads up.'

They continued walking towards the light, taking extra care where they trod. After five minutes Joe again called a halt.

'Anything different, Oliver?'

'No, nothing different.' Oliver was now peering towards the light, which seemed to get bigger as they approached. Just then a shadow seemed to pass in front of the light.

'Movement, boss!' Derek had said it but they all saw it. Was it something alive or a trick of the light? Unlikely to be a trick of the light as they were not all stood together and had three different perspectives on it.

'Weapons free, remember what we have been ordered to do.' All three moved the weapon safety to fire. 'Derek, I want you right behind me with the EDW. Oliver, watch our backs.'

The three men moved forward down into the cave; the light grew bigger until they could make out the irregular edges of the light. Oliver, although at the back, noticed it first.

'That looks just like an entrance to the outside!' Oliver turned to look behind him hoping he could still see the way they had come into the system– he couldn't, of course, way too far back from where they were now.

'Can't be an entrance,' said Joe, looking at the map of the area. 'Even if there is another entrance to the system we would have to have travelling a couple of miles before we got there.'

Just then a figure or something passed across the light – quick but definitely there. Oliver was the first to react, bringing his weapon into the aim in an instant. The shape was gone.

'What do we think that was then?' Joe was also in the aim now but with nothing to shoot at.

'Steady as we go – be careful.' Joe led the way down the cave; the light was brighter and detail was starting to be visible; it looked like they were indeed nearing another entrance. Bright sunlight and vegetation could now be seen past the entrance.

'Wait here, I'll have a look to see what it is.' Joe moved forward, his A4 in the aim. Joe reached the threshold and stepped into the light; he didn't lower his weapon, he just stood there.

'What is happening?' Derek said to Oliver, not really expecting an answer.

'Is that thing ready to go?' asked Oliver, pointing to the EDW that Derek had.

'Sure is, and showing full power available.' Both men were now a little twitchy but neither showed it.

'OK, let's go and see what he has found, be on guard.' Oliver walked slowly towards the entrance where Joe was still standing; he seemed to be staring at something just out of sight to the right of the cave entrance.

Joe turned as Oliver exited the cave. Joe was pleased that Oliver had his weapon pointed directly at him. *Taking no chances just as ordered, good man*, he though. Derek was just inside the entrance; he too had his weapon pointed in Joe's direction; the light on it slowly blinking indicating it was ready to discharge.

It was then that the two men saw what Joe was looking at: Tom and Billy were standing a few feet away in the sunlight; they had been taken by surprise as well so all five had weapons pointing at each other.

'Steady fellas, let's take a step back before it gets too exciting.' Joe was the first to speak, lowering his gun and taking a more relaxed stance. The four followed suit, putting the safety back on.

'Well what was that about then?' Joe was talking. 'We went into the cave, didn't make any turns and now we are back where we started – don't make much sense.'

'Perhaps we were disorientated when we encountered the vibration and simply came back the way we had been,' Oliver suggested.

'No, I was touching or leaning on the cave wall the whole time the vibration was happening; I definitely did not turn round.' Joe's mind was trying to get to grips with what had happened. Had they turned around? Parallel universe? Had the cave system rotated underneath them? He made a mental note: *Stop reading so much science fiction.*

'Did you two feel any sort of vibration or nausea about ten minutes ago?' Joe was addressing Billy and Tom who looked a little puzzled.

'No, nothing, we were preparing the entrance for demolition and then you were there; didn't see or hear you coming.'

'There's something else, Joe.' Billy was looking at his GPS attached to a lanyard around his neck. 'We all seem to have moved; we are not where we were ten minutes ago, according to this we are about half a click further west.' They were all now looking at their GPS.

'Any chance of a malfunction or error with the position?' Joe was looking at the surrounding area; all seemed to be the same as before they entered the cave. Billy began walking away from the group, still looking at the device; he then turned at right angles and began climbing a small outcrop on the valley side. He turned and returned to the group.

'The GPS is seeing all that I just did; it even picked very accurately the change in altitude; by this we have moved four hundred and ten metres from our original position and so has the cave entrance and all this shrubbery etc.'

'Impossible, but we seem to have been moved from the original position. Two impossible thing, then: this and the fact the cave seemed to turn around within the hill while we were in it.' Joe was making notes; he then began putting information into the Pinger, communicating with control. The device beeped once then was silent.

'Now we wait,' Joe said moving over to a small bank of earth that was opposite the cave entrance. 'I suggest we get some rest; at least one of us should be alert and ready at all times.'

It wasn't that any of them were tired but people doing this sort of a job for a living never wasted time doing things that weren't required when they could be resting; too often things would happen that would prevent rest or sleep for some considerable time. Always rest when you can; if there was nothing to do, rest.

12.

Five hundred kilometres away, in Wales, the object was emitting short regular pulses of radiation. The team in the area had noticed this, of course, but could make no more sense of the emissions than before. This time, however, the output was increasing, albeit ever so slowly. It had started about two hours previously at about the time the three men had entered the cave in Ireland. Jonathan had just got the report from Joe; another thing that didn't make sense to add to the list of things that didn't make sense. He would have to think about the team in Ireland and decide what to do; he couldn't leave them there indefinitely.

Jonathan was standing in the control tent watching the instrumentation. 'Is the level still rising?'

'Yes, it is but nowhere near dangerous yet, not even right up next to it. We could be here in a week and still be safe at this rate. The man speaking was new and had only arrived by helicopter about three hours before. *Another expert that has popped out of the woodwork,* thought Jonathan. *Still this is a very big setup with everybody and his uncle taking an interest.*

'Woah! That was interesting.' The man looking at the screens was now peering very closely to the output indication on the left monitor. 'Output has increased, or at least the rate of increase has increased,' he said not looking up.

The graph on the monitor showed a fairly big step with the red line now moving in a more vertical direction than it had been before.

'At this rate we will be having problems in about an hour or so – that's if there are no more steps up in the rate of increase.'

'Right, let's get all non-essential personnel away to site B; we must assume that the levels will get into the dangerous very shortly.' Jonathan was speaking to a man who had been following him around but not saying anything at all; he didn't even acknowledge greetings from any of the other people in the tent.

'Yes, Doctor Smyth.' The man consulted a list he had on a clipboard and looked around the room. 'Only one in here,' he said to himself as he walked over to a technician that was working at a computer on the table in the rear of the tent. The man said something to him and without any hesitation the technician got up and walked out; he didn't take anything with him. The man with the clipboard had a last look around and also left without saying anything.

At least people are remembering the plan that was drilled into them from the start of this operation. The main thing: if you are told to do something, do it.

The object down in the valley was now visible to the naked eye; well just, if the light was right and the observer used off-centre vision. Off-centre vision is a term most who have ever served in any military of any note will be familiar with. If the object that is being viewed is indistinct or in poor light or even darkness don't look directly at it but look to one side. A low-light TV camera could also produce a similar effect by shifting from true colour to black and white. The object had become visible, albeit rather vague, when the radiation output increased some hours before. It was now becoming clearer as time went on but the increase was gradual.

Jonathan went out of the tent and watched several dozen personnel getting onto the transport that would take them to the alternative site some twenty miles away. There was little talk with everyone standing in line waiting for their turn; the man with the clipboard was standing by and double-checking those that were waiting. Once all were aboard the man with the clipboard was the last to get on as the transport moved out onto the road.

Doctor Smyth returned to the tent. 'Any increase on the output?' Jonathan was addressing the man watching the graph. 'Still climbing at the same rate.' The man said without turning round. The screen showed the rate of climb was still in the increased range that had been noted about half an hour ago. *What is this all about?* pondered the doctor.

The moving scale on the instruments stayed the same for just over three hours.

The object in the valley was following its instructions; it could do no other; its sole purpose was to be here and follow the plan. The rotation deadline had approached and passed and it had acted. The result would end in its destruction, but that was only a consequence of the plan it was following. It increased the output.

'Another step up, doctor.' The man at the screen was now fiddling about with the keyboard, calling up more information, trying to find what had increased and what had not. 'There has been a large increase across the spectrum – in the red zone within two hundred metres. If the rise continues at this rate we will be in the red zone in about sixty minutes or so, depending on the ground between us and it.'

'Time to get rid of this thing!' The doctor was speaking so that all in the tent could hear him. 'How long before the EDW is fully powered?'

'Ten seconds.' A technician sitting at the control desk was watching the display. 'Three, two, one… ready to fire doctor.'

The doctor didn't wait; as soon as the technician had finished speaking Jonathan said, '*Fire.*'

Down in the valley it was aware that the weapon they had used against others was powering up but it was not sure why. Was it now a threat? It didn't know so kept to the plan; another increase was imminent.

The very large Electrical Discharge Weapon was setup not far from the object. It had been powered down since it was placed so as to minimise the chances of an attack from the object; it would seem that since the weapon wasn't powered it would not be attacked and so far this seemed to be the case. As the technician gave the command to power up several lights blinked on the control panel that was attached to the side of the weapon. Finally a red light illuminated and started to blink on and off; an indication that the device was ready to discharge. The "fire" command came remotely from the technician up on the top of the valley.

From the EDW, a massive burst of energy erupted and arced towards the object; the output had been increased tenfold since the episode in Oman to make sure that the discharge was overwhelming.

The object watched the discharge coming towards it; time had slowed down to enable it to determine what was happening. It would have to move or it would be destroyed, it concluded, but that would stop the process and the process was an absolute priority and was to be followed no matter what. It had been instructed by the watchers that the alternate plan was to be followed and all in the time it had taken for the discharge to approach it: less than a tenth of a second.

Doctor Smyth and all the staff up on the side of the valley never knew what happened; the object, the EDW, the whole side of the valley, along with everybody on Site A, were vaporised in an instant. Instead a large spherical hole marked its place. At the same time as it was destroyed the object generated an enormous output of radiation all across the spectrum. Curiously there was no blast at all. One second it was there and the next gone; as it all had been scooped out like a piece of ice cream.

All the staff that had been removed from Site A were now settling down at Site B. Professor Bobb was looking over the shoulders of several people working at the control section of the site; here all the information gathered at Site A was repeated. The professor and his team had been watching the telemetry coming over the link; all were eager to see what changed in output when the weapon was fired. All of a sudden the output from Site A ceased.

'What's happened here, Clive?' The professor was talking to the engineer that was responsible for the technical infrastructure of Site B. 'Don't know, we seem to have lost the whole link but that is not possible; there are several different and independent origins for the information. I cannot imagine a circumstance that would turn it all off at the same time.'

'Can we task the drone?'

'Yes, professor, I'm on it now; should be getting telemetry in about five minutes; as luck would have it, came on task about twenty minutes ago.'

A large screen that sat above the other monitors flickered on; the terrain in the valley floor was shown in black and white. 'Should be coming up to the object and Site A anytime now,' the man operating the camera control said.

The drone was flying an elliptical orbit up and down the valley and was controlled by a drone pilot who was not at Site B. The camera, however, was under the control of the man at the desk so any areas of interest within the orbit could be monitored. The camera was stabilised so could fix on a point while the aircraft moved in a wide arc.

'Put it on the main screen,' the professor said, turning around so he was facing a very large screen at the other end of the tent. The screen blinked on then off as the signal arrived from the drone. The picture came on again, this time in colour. What they were all looking at took them by complete surprise. No one spoke but all were staring at the image that was being relayed.

'That is impossible!' The professor was speaking but it was a thought shared by all of those watching. What had been a rocky outcrop on the side of the valley was now gone; a very large spherical depression was now recessed into the valley side. The area where the object had been was about centre to the depression, a large hole with smooth sides and a curved edge. The angle of view slowly changed as the drone made its pass and began to turn across the valley for the upward leg of the orbit. They could now see the hole from the other side, a position directly above where Site A should have been. There was no smoke, no debris, nothing at all.

The technician switched to infrared, anticipating a command the professor was about to give; any hot spots, or indeed cold spots, would now show up. No unusually hot or cold areas; everything in the crater was the same ambient temperature as the surrounding area with just a few slight variations. The crater looked like it had always been there and not scooped out ten minutes before.

'That is impossible!' The professor said again.

'Someone down there, professor!' The technician was speaking while staring intently at the screen on his desk. The rest of them were looking at the large screen and had seen the same thing. There appeared to be a single person that was stood at the edge of the crater.

'Can we get a better picture from this angle?' The drone was moving away on its circuit so the technician had to demand maximum zoom to keep the image quality the same. As the image cleared the figure turned and seemed to look directly at the camera; the drone at this stage would have been a couple of miles away, most people would be unlikely even to see it in the air.

The drone was now making the turn at the end of the circuit; it would be moving down the opposite leg in a few moments and would fly very close to the figure in the valley, albeit some distance above it.

The picture on the small monitor as well as the large screen showed someone standing at the edge of the crater. The picture was now getting very clear as the distance closed.

'Can we get the thermal onto that?' The professor asked.

The image changed to one of false colours highlighting hot as red and cold as blue.

'Normal output for a clothed human who is not exercising, professor.' The technician was wandering why he had said that as it was obviously a clothed human who was indeed stood still.

The drone was now at its closest point so they could all see the man who was on the ground looking directly at them; he was dressed in dark-coloured trousers, a tee shirt and was wearing boots. He was looking directly at the camera and gave the impression that he could see them looking at him; the technician was not alone in thinking that it was all a bit odd.

'That is the missing STT bloke!' A man at the back of the tent was talking.

'Indeed it is,' said the professor.

The professor had only met Big Dave on the one occasion after the initial entry team had finished their briefing but it was hard to forget a man of Big Dave's size and bearing. The man on the ground was unmistakably Dave who everyone believed was dead, vaporised in the valley leaving no trace.

Now he was back; looking well and undamaged but not doing anything except look at the drone, only shifting his position as the drone moved around the circuit.

'We need to get a team there to have a look at this fellow.' The professor was speaking to the control representative who was stood by the door.

'Not yet, professor, we have still to complete the survey of the anomaly.' The man was matter-of-fact but left no doubt that it would be his decision if anybody went down the valley to have a look at this "fellow". The survey was about halfway through and involved several ground vehicles and, of course, the drone; as well as carrying the camera, the drone was equipped with all manner of sensory equipment but at this time the information coming back was not telling them anything. There was no residual radiation or anything out of the ordinary in the valley, only Big Dave. The professor loved the way these people called an unknown "the anomaly".

Big Dave was a little puzzled. It seemed that one minute he was in total darkness on the smooth floor, wherever that was, and the next he was here. He wondered where Tom and Joe had got to; they weren't that far away when he had seen the flash of light. To him it had been overwhelming, so they must have seen it. As for the dark room with a smooth floor and walls that followed you around, who knows? He was getting a little more focussed, however; his training was kicking in. *Don't concern yourself with what was, concentrate on what is now.* But what was now? He was stood on the edge of a depression that he was sure was not there before, a depression that looked like it had been scooped out by a giant spoon; perhaps it had been dressed after excavation he thought. Where was all the spoil? There were no tracks on the ground to indicate that any heavy machinery had been this way. Then there was the drone; how did he notice that? Drones were almost invisible to the naked eye at the altitudes they were operated at. There had been many a "target" that had been destroyed by a drone-launched missile without ever knowing it was even there, yet he could clearly see it and noticed it straight away. His or anybody else's eyesight was not that good. Well it never used to be anyway. He also knew somehow that he was the subject of interest for this drone.

The professor was now waving at the security to attract attention. 'Major, we will be moving to the mobile control centre as soon as is practicable; get some men down there and pick him up when you can. Quick as you like, major.'

'Yes, professor; the chopper is available now.'

Both men turned and strode out of the tent. The professor was now moving a lot faster than was normal – an indication that he was moving the plan forward at a pace. As he walked over to the helicopter line, which had three helicopters waiting, he noticed that one was already running up with four or five men in black clothing sitting inside. By the time he had reached the edge of the line the chopper lifted off and headed down the valley to where Big Dave was still standing. The professor was met by a crewman, who handed him a headset. 'We are all ready to go, professor, please sit on the right facing rear.' The crewman made sure his passenger was seated correctly then closed the side door and said something to the pilot that the professor couldn't quite hear. The engines increased in noise and the chopper lifted off. The professor sat back and closed his eyes; he had a lot to think about.

13.

The Pinger on Joe's arm beeped once and a dull green light illuminated. Joe immediately looked at it and noticed the message had come from Site B. He read it several times and sat upright.

'We have to try again but only one more time; either way we will end this today.' Joe got to his feet as the rest were doing the same. All adjusted their kit and made sure they were ready.

'Same as last time; I will lead and followed by Derek – make sure that thing is ready to go – and, Oliver, you take up the rear. Tom and Billy will stay outside. Only problem here is that this is not the point we entered the cave; according to all our navigation stuff we are about a click from the entry point. However, the demolition charges are here in the cave entrance so it appears that half the side of the hill has moved along with us all. Ideas?' Joe was doing the right thing; there was no immediate need to launch so why not get a consensus. Billy was checking the charge that was at the entrance to the cave. 'Looks just like the ones I placed first as you three went into the cave; this has even got my knot on it.' Billy was referring to a type of slipknot his grandfather had shown him when he was a boy at school; he had used it many times since on all manner of attachments. It worked very well and could be released very quickly, if you knew what you were doing. 'Unless my granddad is here, I tied this knot, no question.'

'I think we should ignore the satnav info and take this as the same cave; it could be that the satnav is in error. I'm sure we have all had problems with this particular piece of technology before; ground radar systems sometimes affect them, although I'm not sure if there is any ground radar transmitting around here.' Tom was saying what they all thought; better here than half a click up the valley only to find that there is nothing there. 'All agreed then?' Tom didn't think there would be any better ideas as the options were fairly limited: stay here or walk up the valley where they thought the cave actually was, even though they all stood in front of it right here.

'Right, two things can happen from now: one, we enter the cave and the same thing happens, in which case we destroy the entrance and evacuate, and, two, we find something in there and then we destroy it and the cave. Any questions?'

All five were ready and no one had a question. Joe led the way into the cave with Derek about ten feet behind, with Oliver as the last one in. The two outside checked the charges again, then moved into the cave with the fuel/air bomb and placed it about fifteen feet from the entrance. Then they retraced their steps and took up a firing position at right angle to the cave entrance behind a large outcrop of granite about thirty feet from the cave.

Joe picked up the pace a little quicker than before; time was short and this had to resolve one way or the other. They reached the place they had experienced the nausea the time before. Nothing happened.

'OK, we are here and all is well; what next?' Joe was speaking to the other two but not really expecting an answer.

'Let's get on while the going is good.' Oliver was speaking from a few yards behind; he had kept his distance from the lead just in case. Derek was in between him and Joe again, obeying the rules and ready with the EDW.

Joe stepped off again but as soon as he moved the cave walls seemed to be convulsing again along with the vibration and nausea. A rerun of the time before but this time it wasn't giving up. All three were on the ground curled with their hands on their ears to try and block out whatever it was.

Suddenly the cave was still and the vibration ceased.

'Was that the same as last time, Oliver?' Joe was asking as he got to his feet.

'Yes, but a lot more intense.' Oliver was rubbing his eyes to try and clear his head.

'On we go,' Joe said as he got up and moved off in the same direction as before; at least they all thought it was the same direction – they did last time and look where that got them.

Right on cue the light at the end of the tunnel appeared and just in front was the fuel/air bomb that the other two had set up.

'Looks like a rerun of the last time,' Joe said. Let's get ready to close this cave and get out of here.'

As they moved of the vibration returned and the end of the tunnel and the fuel/air bomb vanished to be replaced by the tunnel walls that disappeared into the darkness.

'This is getting interesting.' The comment came from Derek who was now looking at the weapon he carried; the control panel no longer showed the ready light but instead showed that the weapon was powering up from off, which shouldn't have been happening as the weapon was charged and ready to go before they entered the cave; it should have remained at ready for at least two hours before cycling.

Joe and Oliver were now looking at the control panel.

'OK, let's prioritise; the first thing we need to do is get out of here, we can go and beat up the manufacturer of that thing when we get the opportunity.'

Joe was now looking back down the cave the way they had come – if indeed they had come that way and this wasn't another complication put on them by God knows who.

'If that thing keeps playing up remove the power unit and ditch the rest,' Joe said in a way that didn't invite comment.

'Problem here, boss.' Derek was still looking at the control panel. 'It is continuing to charge and is well into the red; not long before we have an automatic discharge or it will go belly up-big style, either way it won't be good for us.

Oliver was on the weapon in an instant; using his combat knife he sawed through a large cable that ran from the battery to the control unit as he did this there was a sound of electrical shorting and a very large flash of light; Derek and Oliver were both thrown to the ground; a acrid smell of burning hung in the air. Oliver got to his feet and offered his hand to Derek, who didn't take it but got up on his own.

'Sorry about that, mate, but it was better than the high-voltage bit discharging with us right next to it.'

'What do you mean? Weren't "we" going to discharge the thing any way if we encountered something to shoot at?' Derek was a little pissed off, both Joe and Oliver could see that.

'Only good for stabbing now, methinks.' Oliver was looking at his knife; a large part of the blade was gone.

'Never mind that, why did you not want to let the weapon discharge in here when the plan was to do just that?' Joe had joined the conversation and seemed as irritable as Derek.

'The weapon was not going to discharge, as you put it, it was on the way to a catastrophic overload; the output from it would have killed us all in an instant and we would not have been able to direct it. I saved all our lives; I think you should recommend me for a gong at least.' Oliver was trying to make light of a very serious situation.

'How come you suddenly know an awful lot about the EDW?' Joe asked.

'Some things I pick up very quickly – a natural talent I suppose – I just remember trivia.'

'Good job you did, now let's get going. Ditch that thing– it's not a lot of use to us now Oliver has cut it up.' Joe was already walking down the cave system the way they had come. Joe didn't think for a minute that they owed their lives to a bloke who just happened to remember things and then find the information in a matter of life or death. All that could wait; priorities of action: if it can be left waiting, let it wait.

Joe had picked up the pace and it wasn't long before they exited the cave and were stood in the open with the other two. They confirmed what Joe was thinking; they had not noticed anything strange this time, same as the last. Only in the cave was anything different. Joe had considered that they were, in fact, not even out of the cave but somewhere else. However, that had become all too difficult and had implications that were all too scary.

'Let's all get behind the firing position and do this.' Joe and the rest of them moved quickly and all now stood behind the granite outcrop.

'Go for it, Tom,' Joe indicated that the time had come.

Tom removed the safety from the firing box and pressed the command button. There was a short delay as the programme started; first the fuel/air device would initiate then the cave entrance would be brought down. Both detonations seemed to come together but the bomb inside the cave was momentarily in front of the other. The result was a massive explosion that literally brought the side of the valley down over where the cave entrance had been a moment before. A large cloud of dust was blowing out into the valley. It was accompanied by a deep and lasting rumbling sound that must have heard for miles in all directions.

'We had better get the hell out of here before someone pitches up to see what the noise is all about.' Joe was using the Pinger to get a helicopter in and hopefully get them all out of here.

Joe led the way as they collected their gear and moved up the side of the valley towards the extraction point. Joe set a very quick pace but they were all able to keep up. No one wanted to be left behind on this one, too many strange things going on.

14.

They made the top of the valley in good time and then moved over to a sheltered area beside a large gorse bush that was clinging to the side of some rock outcrops. By the way the bush had grown, it was clear that the winds in this place were often quite severe. From their position, they could see into the valley and just about make out the collapsed cave area that was now about two miles away in direct line of sight. The smoke from the demolition still hung in the air and was slowly drifting away down the valley as the wind picked up then died off again. The weather had changed quite a bit from when they had arrived in the valley and was becoming quite pleasant. Tom took out his binoculars and began scanning the area, just to make sure they were alone and that the explosion had not attracted any unwanted attention from the locals. There seemed to be nothing happening down the whole length of the valley, at least not in the bits he could see from this high vantage point. He settled his view on the place they had just rearranged with the explosives charges. What he saw was a little confusing: the dust where the cave entrance had been was moving around in circles as if a local wind eddy was playing tricks.

'Tom, have a look at this. What do you think it is?' He passed the binoculars to Tom who sat down and rested his elbows on his knees. Sure enough, the dust was behaving as if something was blowing it around but only in a small area.

'Could just be the wind moving up the valley and creating eddies because of the rocky outcrop we sheltered behind when we blew it.' Tom was still looking and not at all sure his explanation was correct. The dust now appeared to be moving up the side of the valley and then down again, all very slowly and not reducing in size. Then the whole area seemed to blur and the mound of rock and earth that had been dislodged to seal the cave was gone; in its place was the cave entrance, reformed and exactly as they had found it all those hours ago.

'This is getting weird!' Tom said as he passed the binoculars back to Joe. 'Have a look at that.'

The others were now interested and all gathered round sharing the other two sets of binoculars between them.

'Even with a digger it would have taken a couple of days to dig that lot out and I reckon to get it back as was would be nigh on impossible.' Billy was talking now but he was saying what they all thought. It was now apparent that the whole valley side and the cave had been restored to pre-demolition.

'Is the cave in the original or the second position?' Tom directed the question to Oliver who was busy with his satnav.

'A far as I can tell from here it is in the original position, so in effect it has followed us out of the valley.'

The Pinger on Joe's arm beeped once. 'It seems one of our mates has turned up.'

Joe read the message again and looked up. 'Big Dave has appeared at the first site in the valley, seemingly unharmed but not doing anything except stare at the drone that is flying around.'

'What?' Tom was getting up to have a look at the display as if he didn't believe what Joe was saying.

'Look for yourself,' Joe said offering the display to Tom.

The short line of text described briefly what had happened in the Welsh valley.

The Pinger beeped once more and displayed another message; they were to be extracted within the next twenty minutes and return to Wales.

They all took the time to rearrange their equipment, a habit they had all acquired from previous outings on similar operations – maybe not too similar, but habits were formed doing this sort of job that didn't go away very easily. Joe again wondered at the way Billy and Oliver Glapton seemed to merge with the rest of the team; they had obviously not pursued an exclusively academic career; the story about being Royal Marines reserves didn't quite explain their polished professionalism.

The Pinger made a sound. 'Problem!' Joe said looking at the display. 'We are not at the extraction point; the chopper is there and we are not.'

They all compared the GPS figures; all agreed that they were indeed at the pickup point but the helicopter was not with them. Joe had replied to the message as they were confirming their location; the Pinger sounded again.

'We have been left for the time being as the chopper couldn't loiter.' Joe was a little irritated now; he had never in his whole career been confused to his own whereabouts – embarrassing!

'Something odd going on, boss.' Oliver was speaking looking up at the sun, which was a few degrees above the horizon. 'When we got here the valley was running just about east to west but now it seems that it runs north to south.' He demonstrated his reckoning by checking the time and the position of the sun. Sure enough they were on the valley side just short of the summit but the valley was running in a different direction to when they had arrived.

'The valley is moving and our ride hasn't turned up, can't remember reading about this sort of situation in the books.' Tom was now checking his compass against GPS. 'Yep, we are on the valley side but not facing the way we should be; are we sure this is the same valley?' The rest nodded in agreement, each of them doing the calculation and checking the position of the sun.

'Soon be dark,' Derek remarked.

'Alternate pickup point it is then,' Joe said as he looked at his GPS again. The problem might be determining in which direction they should move; the alternate pickup point was two miles due west of their position at the moment – at least it was two miles from where they thought they all were.

'OK, let's assume that the GPS and our own dead reckoning are at fault here; what is the constant that is unlikely to be giving us wrong information?' It was a rhetorical question of course; all five of them knew that the only thing that could not be wrong was the setting sun, which was about to disappear over the valley edge opposite them, after that it would be the stars, if they could see any, when it got dark. To go two miles due west from where they were meant a decent into the valley and out over the far crest. It would be truly dark by the time they made the far ridge and then around a mile and a half to the next pickup point, which should be on a level area not far from a small wood.

'All ready? Time to move, let's make the best time we can and get out of this godforsaken place. Soon be back in Wales.'

They moved at quite a pace down into the valley they had left an hour or so ago; all looked the same as before and the going was fairly easy. Once at the bottom it was a short move along the valley floor until they reached the obvious route to the top on the other side. Billy and Oliver were again showing impressive stamina as they tackled the other side of the valley;

it wasn't as steep as the side they had come down but it was hard going all the same. They reached the top in about twenty minutes from start. The landscape stretched out before them. The sun had now gone down but twilight persisted and gave them a reasonable view of the terrain in front of them. There were to be no more valleys between them and the secondary pickup point so it should be straightforward.

'The extraction point is about one and a half clicks from here so we should be there in around twenty minutes depending on the going.' Joe took a last look at the Pinger and set off towards the point where the sun had gone down.

The pace set by Joe was brisk but no one had the need to break into a jog; all the rest were able to keep pace without too much effort. The ground did seem to be very flat and not too wet so the distance was eaten up very quickly. None of the men said anything while they moved; all were keeping to the training they had received in previous outings. They had been trained in at least three different places and times but all kept to a standard way of operating and were easily recognised for what they were: military professionals.

'We're here,' Joe said squatting down and looking at the Pinger again. 'Chopper will be on us in about five minutes, let's get all our kit ready to go.'

Each one took their day sacks and other items off and bundled them ready to push onto the aircraft. The chopper would likely have no seats in it so the packs and other equipment could serve as a seat for the trip back to Wales. The Blackhawk was on them before they knew, swooping in very low from the east. It had flown from an aircraft carrier that had been sitting in international waters out in the Atlantic. The crew had been ready to go for a couple of hours and had replaced the aircraft that had originally launched to pick the team up on the first attempt. The pilot was half thinking that the team was lost and even this time they wouldn't be here. He was wrong; the group was exactly where they should have been.

The five-man team crouched, ready to get onto the helicopter when the load master signalled them. Thumbs-up from the crewman in the side door. Joe led the team towards the helicopter. Once at the side the crewman assisted them to get their kit and themselves into the main cargo compartment. There were no seats as they had expected. Joe sat facing rear with his back against the bulkhead; Billy was next to him with the other three against the opposite wall of the compartment. The loadmaster was standing, talking to the pilot. Within two minutes of landing the aircraft was airborne and heading out towards the Atlantic; the helicopter showed no lights and kept very low.

The watchers observed the team leave; they expected that they would explore a little longer in the valley but the team had gone at the same time as all the others. Perhaps they too worked to a plan dictated by others.

'Five minutes.' The pilot announced over the intercom; they had been in the air for about half an hour already and Joe was a little surprised they were so far out and he had expected an American voice but this one was definitely Irish, probably Belfast.

More importantly, they were not going to Wales!

15.

The helicopter banked suddenly and then levelled out, a couple of seconds later the nose lifted as the aircraft flared to reduce forward speed and then they were on deck. The side door opened and the five-man team were marshalled out and over towards an open door in the side of the carrier's island.

'Good evening, gentlemen. I am Commander Brown, United States Navy, please let these men take your kit and weapons, you are needed at the briefing session, please follow me.'

The commander strode off down the passageway; the five men followed. It wasn't long before they were confronted by a closed bulkhead door complete with an armed marine guard. The marine acknowledged the commander and opened the door. All six were now in a medium-sized conference room with only two doors; the one they had entered by and another on the opposite wall.

'Make yourself comfortable, gentlemen; please wait here for the professor to arrive, we expect him in around two hours. Chow is over there and the washrooms are through the far door. Please don't leave this compartment.'

The compartment was about thirty feet by thirty and contained three rows of seats that were facing a blank screen on one bulkhead. There was no one else in the room but along one side were tables that had various types of food laid out. A large electric boiler was steaming away in the corner.

Billy and Oliver were the first to go and look at what was on offer at the food table; Derek went through to the washroom.

'What is going on now, Joe? Tom was the first to speak.

'Don't know, mate, probably a debriefing with the professor, assuming it is Professor Bobb and not some other one.' Joe was watching the Glapton brothers; they were sat down eating and chatting in the far corner. It did appear that they knew what was going on and he didn't; mildly irritating but hey ho, don't concern yourself with imagined or possible problems. Derek returned and sat in one of the seats at the front and promptly went to sleep.

Joe and Tom continued to speculate on what would be the outcome of their little expedition to Ireland.

'What was that little journey all about?' Tom said scratching his head.

'Don't know but we have wasted a lot of time and resources to find nothing; this thing we are now on for instance, what is it doing here? We have an awful lot of assets following us around. There must be some big effort involving many agencies to generate this level of support.' Joe was no more in the picture than the rest of them, *except maybe the Glaptons*, he thought. Still not sure about those two, he made a decision to ask Professor Bobb what they were about – that's if the professor turned up.

'For now, food and rest.' Joe got up and walked over to the food.

The aircraft carrier was vibrating indicating that the vessel was working up to full speed. 'We are going somewhere fast,' Tom said to himself. These Nimitz-class carriers – Joe thought it was a Nimitz but could be one of the more modern ones – could get to more than thirty knots if pushed and judging by the vibration it was being pushed.

The carrier was indeed a Nimitz-class vessel; the USS *Ronald Reagan* was now at full speed and was making in excess of thirty knots, heading due south. The sea was calm and the wind had subsided; perfect high-speed steaming weather. The *Ronald Reagan* had to be at the second pickup area in an hour and would easily make it on time.

Another Blackhawk was making its final approach to the carrier; the lights were on and they were good to land. They had been in the air for a couple of hours and the four-man team in the back were all asleep. The crewman gave the team leader a shake to let him know they were close. The team leader nodded and gave the other three a push to wake them up. He put his finger in the air and drew a circle to indicate they were about to move.

The helicopter landed in the same place that Joe's transport had touched down an hour or so previously. The four men were marshalled in the same manner as before: the same commander and the same route to the conference room. They were shown in but without any introduction. The door was closed behind them.

Joe recognised the first one through the door immediately: John Flett who he worked with on more than one occasion in some of the worst places on the planet. A very capable bloke in Joe's opinion but he would never say that to him.

'John Flett! What are you doing here? I thought this was a party for the good guys.'

Joe was joking, of course. John Flett was certainly one of the good guys and had proven as much many times. Joe went over and shook his hand; he then introduced the rest of the team starting with Tom and the Glapton brothers; Derek was snoring away in the corner. John Flett did the same and it soon transpired that they were all much the same and had been two teams doing a similar job. Similarly, the job in the end hadn't made any sense. Both teams had experienced the land orientation moving and then returning to its original position. Both groups of men agreed that they were all involved in something really odd. John Flett's team had been in Cornwall, out on Bodmin Moor experiencing very similar events; odd radiation source, ground seemingly moving and the land orientation at odds with what they first encountered.

'Who are we waiting for?' John Flett was talking to Joe.

'Not sure, we think it is Professor Bobb but could be some other professor; have to wait and see. We are to be debriefed I assume and then get an idea of what they want of us. We are obviously not going home tonight.'

The nine men had been in the conference room for over six hours and were making the most of the food and the opportunity to rest; the majority had removed most of their clothing and had taken their boots off, all were resting with their feet up.

The door opened and in walked Professor William Bobb; with him was Lily Gamosk and a second man carrying a large attaché case. Joe didn't recognise him and he was sure he hadn't met the individual before. The professor walked to the front of the room and turned to face the men who were now stirring, even Derek was awake. Lily and the second man remained at the back of the room.

'Gentlemen, thank you for being patient, I imagine it has been somewhat confusing for you all over the last couple of days.' The professor paused.

'Just to recap on what has been said at previous meetings with us and others regarding the chain of events that have led us here to this room.'

The professor outlined what had happened so far and reminded them all that it was thought that something was at work trying to alter the Earth's magnetic field; he thought that there was no direct evidence that the cylinder had anything to do with the state of Mars as it was today and that the object discovered in orbit around Venus was unexplained. However, he did remind them that circumstantial evidence pointed to the objects found on Earth being connected to the reduction of the Earth's magnetic field. He then reminded both teams about what they had been up to in Ireland and Cornwall over the last day or so. Both had entered a cave system and both had been confounded by the events that followed; moving tunnels and moving land mass.

'Why did this happen to you? Well we think we are being deceived or misdirected in both locations. It is now thought that there was nothing in either Ireland or the south-west of England but our attention had been drawn there to waste time and effort. Since you left to come here all radiation signatures from both sites have ceased. That is, as soon as we lost interest whatever it was that causing theses readings stopped. By the way, you are not the only teams out there looking for these radiation signatures; we have ten teams in all, everyone has had the same results. So there was quite a lot of effort chasing shadows and quite significantly, in my opinion, no one was injured or lost during these forays.'

The professor checked a notebook he had and continued.

'There was one very big incident that you are not aware of; the site in Wales that was the control of the encounter that Tom and company experienced is no longer there. The whole site and everything and everybody in it have gone. Everything went when we tried to destroy the object in the valley; we used the normal large-output EDW as we have done before but this time as the weapon was fired everything was removed. There was no blast or sound generated, it was as if the whole basin in the area of the site was scooped out: no debris, nothing left. We will pause here to let Brian set up the display.'

He motioned to the man with the case at the back of the room to come forward.

'Gentlemen, I would like to introduce Brian Gates; he is one of our team of very clever people that is helping us in this endeavour.'

Brian nodded to the audience and set up a small device about the size of a laptop on a small table at the front of the room. He switched it on and an opening page with *START* in bold flashed onto the wall. He went back to the rear of the room next to Lily.

'When I said there was nothing left behind at the site I was not completely accurate, Brian.' He nodded at Brian who was holding a remote for the projector.

An aerial view of Site A came onto the screen; what the professor had told them had not prepared them for the sheer scale of the hole now residing where the site had been.

'That is amazing.' John Flett said what they were all thinking.

'Yes, John it is truly amazing but there is more to come.' The professor indicated to change the slide.

This time a moving picture was displayed; an aerial picture that was taken from an aircraft moving up the valley. They were all soon able to see a figure stood at the edge of the very large hole; it appeared to be motionless and looking at the camera. The image zoomed in so that they could all see that it was a man and a man they some of them recognised.

'Yes, gentlemen, that is David Smith – Big Dave, as you know him. It definitely is; he has been retrieved and will be on his way here as soon as we debrief him. He is at present in a location in France. Currently we don't know how he went, where he went or how he got back but hopefully we will soon.'

The professor then asked each team in turn about what they had experienced in Ireland and Cornwall; both accounts were remarkably similar and the only major difference was the location.

'Very interesting but not wholly unexpected, gentlemen; we have now had around ten expeditions to these anomalies and all but one has come up with the same result. Your two teams were the last in a series of investigations that have been conducted over the last week or so. I'm sure that you have all discussed the moving ground and the disorientation effects that have happened to you all.'

'Right, what is going on, professor?' Joe was speaking for all of them; if they already had an idea about what was to happen, why were the nine of them sent out to possible danger and collect information that even they wouldn't believe if they hadn't been there and seen it.

'Gentlemen, we did not take the decision to send your teams into the unknown lightly but we did consider that there would be little or no danger to you once you encountered whatever it was that was there. Previously we have had the exact same results: lots of strange things going on but not a single casualty. It would appear that whatever it is that is doing this does not want to hurt us.'

The professor was looking at Lily who was still at the back of the room. 'Lily, please come and brief us on what you and your team have discovered over the past couple of weeks.'

Weeks? Joe thought to himself. *We had a briefing from the very same Lily a couple of days ago, did she not give the whole story?*

Lily answered Joe's unspoken question at the start. 'Gentlemen, some of you were at the briefing which I was a part of at Site A in Wales not so long ago. However, I can now tell you some more detail of what we are facing, or at least what we think we are facing and what we might do about it.'

Lily went over the whole story again from the first encounter to the findings on Mars and the object in orbit around Venus. She talked briefly about what had been the effects of the various weapons that had been used against the objects on Earth and finally gave quite a bit more detail regarding the object that had disappeared with half the hillside in Wales.

'The object in Wales that Tom and Derek encountered does seem to be the same but different in many ways. Firstly it was not visible to the naked eye and did not emit any radiation in the non-visible spectrum. It did give bursts of X-rays but only for short periods; the team that Tom led into the valley encountered this as well, of course. There was, however, a physical presence to the object and it could be felt if touched. The output of radiation when we attacked it with the heavy output EDW was completely off the scale but again only for a very short period. The mechanism that enabled it to disappear and take half the valley with it is not understood; there was no debris and no residual radiation. Just like David we do not know where the material and personnel have gone or how they went.

'In a moment the professor will outline the plan so we can move forward from this; at the moment we are fairly certain what is happening on a global scale but have no idea how or why it is happening.'

Nalia Gamosk sat down at the front of the room.

The professor rose and folded his arms. 'Well, here we are; this next couple of weeks I suspect will not be easy and I am not at all sure we will resolve this matter in a manner that we would like. First of all we have to wait for the information that our friend David will provide; perhaps we will gain an insight into the problem that only he can give us. There are other elements to this that we can cover later on when we brief on the next phase. What you all need to do now is get cleaned up and get some rest; at the moment it is planned to have

David here by the morning – about twelve hours away – if he is not ready by then we will delay. A man will be here shortly to show you all to your accommodation on board this fine vessel.'

16.

The navy commander had reappeared and was as talkative as the last time; Joe was used to this as it was standard procedure for the crew of a vessel that was hosting any kind of special ops not to be in contact with the operatives for more than was strictly necessary. They also didn't pass many crewmen and those that were evident stood out of the way and avoided eye contact. They were led down several decks onto what was probably an aircraft hangar deck except that there was a large accommodation building sitting in the middle. It looked like it had been plucked from a field at some construction site on land.

'This is your accommodation, gentlemen. Everything you need for the time being is inside; please do not venture from this facility. Should you require anything extra, please use the telephone that is inside the living area. Chow will be delivered to you. A guard is posted here to maintain your privacy; I will collect you when the professor is ready to continue.'

They all moved into the structure, which was quite substantial; obviously not part of the carrier and had probably been brought down on the aircraft lift into the hangar deck. There was a large seating area with a very large flat screen TV and a work area that had tea and coffee making items. There was a large boiler hissing away that was attached to the wall over the sink. Off the main room was a row of doors that led to ten sleeping compartments, each with a single bed, cupboard space and yet another TV.

'Well, Joe, what are we going to do next? It all seems to have fallen off the table as far as planning goes, unless there is a master plan but we haven't been told the detail yet.' John Flett was obviously getting a little irritated with the waiting around.

'I think that it would be a good idea to get a shower and have a sleep for now; not much point in speculation because so far it has been a very weird trip.' Joe was now looking for a mug in the drawers that were under the counter at the tea station.

'Who's for coffee? Tea?'

The nine men split up and made the best of what was on offer; eating, showering and generally getting cleaned up. It wasn't long before most of them had got into bed and gone to sleep. Joe, Tom and John were sat around the table talking about what had transpired over the last weeks. John Flett explained that he and his team had been doing very similar work to Joe and Tom but that he didn't know until today that his team was not the only one.

'How many more teams do you think they have out there, Joe?'

'Don't know but I'm willing to bet we are a very small part of the whole; perhaps we will find out more when the professor has got some information from Big Dave.'

The professor didn't get back to them for three days; they were starting to get a little agitated because there are only so many movies you can watch end to end without going mad. The group had exhausted small talk and Joe was still not fully sure about Billy and Oliver; he did try and quiz them about their background but they seemed to deal only in generalities.

There was a knock on the door, which then opened

without waiting for a response; the professor came in and said, 'Good morning, gentlemen, I hope you all rested.'

Joe had actually thought that it was mid-afternoon but didn't care too much as it seemed they were now moving on. It would be nice to see the sky again and feel the sun on his face.

'Gentlemen, we are now ready for the next phase and hopefully this will be the last phase also; we will continue the briefing up in the conference facility when you are ready; you only need to bring yourselves so you can leave any excess kit here, I'm sure it will be safe.'

The professor was the first out of the door; the rest followed, eager to find out what they would be expected to do from then on. The same navy commander was waiting outside the door. He said something to the professor that the rest could not hear, turned on his heel and walked off in the direction they had arrived from days before. Joe noticed that the last in line was an armed Marine sentry.

They were now back in the conference room sat in the same chairs as before; the professor was at the front. Lily and Brian were not in the room.

The professor raised his arms to request quiet and began to speak. 'We think we are a little nearer to finding out what is going and for what purpose; the debriefing of David Smith has not yielded as much information as would we had hoped, however he did gain some insight into what may be going on. David did tell us that when he approached the position of the object his radiation warning blipped so he made ready the EDW. At this moment he was only aware of a very brief flash of light that seemed to come from all around him. He then woke up on a very smooth floor but was in total darkness. He also said that the walls of the place he was in appeared to follow him around. Rather like you would expect a spider to feel if trapped under a glass with someone moving it as the spider moved about.'

The professor paused before he continued. 'He has no real idea of how long he was in this position but it ended as it had begun with a similar flash of light, which was painfully bright as he had been in total darkness for some time. The light was short-lived; when his eyes adjusted to the light that followed he was standing on the edge of the large hole that had been Site A.'

The professor went on to explain what had come out of the debrief so far.

'Some things from David are, however, very interesting; he seemed to know about your exploits in Cornwall, Ireland and the other places, he also said that the strange goings on are no direct threat to us. I'm afraid we differ on that small point; all evidence so far indicates that there is a substantial threat at many levels. We asked him how he knew all this but he genuinely doesn't know. He has also undergone some physical changes while he has been away. We compared him to his last medical assessment that was done about a month ago. His eyesight in particular is now markedly different from what it was; he now not only has perfect vision but can also distinguish detail at considerable ranges. All his motor functions are now at a perfect level as if he has been reset to an earlier age. He has absolutely no recollection of anything being done to him and can only remember being in total darkness with a wall that seemed to follow him around.'

'Is he telling us the whole truth, professor?' Tom was sure that Big Dave would be very cooperative but asked the question anyway; it was bound to come up.

'Yes, the debrief team do believe him; he has not been at all uncooperative and has spent quite some time in the process, he even agreed to questioning whilst under hypnosis. Nothing came from that except the dark room with moving walls. Obviously something has happened to him but he cannot recall it. However, there is a far more significant difference to David that the team initially missed.'

The door opened and Lily came followed by Brian who was carrying his little projection device. Lily sat down at the front and Brian set up his little box in the same manner as before.

I wonder why they don't leave that thing here; or use the one that is fixed to the wall at the back of the room. Joe was thinking.

'Gentlemen, I would like Brian to carry on for a little while, after which we will let Lily speak. Brian.' The professor nodded to Brian who stood up and went to the front.

'Good morning, gentlemen, for those that do not know me I am part of a team that monitors all operatives within the system – that is all of you and everybody that is now part of the team. We look after your welfare from an operational point of view; we are normally unnoticed and carry out our work in the background. As some of you may remember when you first started in this business and every subsequent year you are required to undergo a range of medical and physical assessments; this includes a genetic profile that looks at several markers in your genetic makeup. Why do we do this? Well we do exclude individuals that have some of the major defect markers that might lead to problems whilst you are out in the field.'

Brian paused to gauge the response from the audience; this testing had not been advertised previously and anyone rejected because of the tests were not told why but simply informed they did not make the grade for a variety of other reasons.

'Obviously we had David's profile on record so during the debrief sessions we had a look at his genetic profile again and compared it to the one when he was employed. We ran the test several times as we could not quite believe what we found.'

Both teams were now very interested. Where was this going?

'We believe that David is not the same man that went missing in the Welsh valley.'

17.

Brian waited for a few seconds and carried on. 'As some of you may know the human genome can indicate whereabouts the blood line came from on Earth; generally speaking the ascent of man started in East Africa and eventually spread throughout the world. Other species were assimilated into the current genetic profile we all carry. The Neanderthal human gives us, in Europe and some parts of the Far East, about two per cent of our genetic makeup. Other groups carry information from a group recently recognised as Denisovans, a subgroup of the Neanderthal discovered in Siberia. This group is mainly in South East Asia and the Australian continent.

'Our friend David had, at his previous review, a genetic makeup that all of us in this room share; ninety-eight per cent Homo sapiens and two per cent Neanderthal.'

Brian flashed a series of graphs onto the wall.

'This is the genetic profile of David recorded about a year ago. This is the one that was sequenced two days ago.'

'They look the same,' Tom said peering at the detail that was displayed.

'They do look similar but there is a difference that might not be obvious at first sight.' Brian was using a pointer to indicate what he was talking about.

'Look at this, a small indication that the Neanderthal

element is present, as I said before about two per cent of the whole. Now compare that with the recent sequence. The Neanderthal element is not there but has been replaced with a, as yet, unidentified part of the sequence. We have compared it with all ancient DNA we have but have come up with no matches. We do assume that it may be from an ancient human or a hybrid of several ancient humans; it has often been speculated that other human subspecies existed but so far we haven't found DNA material from them. Essentially, gentlemen, the subject is not the same David Smith that was taken from the valley.'

'What are we saying? Is this David a modified David or a completely different David?' All the team were now interested in the question that Joe had just asked.

'We are not sure; he does seem to know everything that the original knew but we are assuming that he is a different David so therefore he will not be joining us as we originally planned. We have to assume that he is a threat until we can confirm that he isn't. He will remain at the facility in France for the time being.'

'Of course we will let you all know when anything else concerning David comes out from the investigation; I know that many of you knew him personally and considered him a friend.' The professor had taken over the lead from Brian.

'From now on, gentlemen, anyone who has had contact with any of the anomalies will be viewed with a little suspicion. You may have noticed that an armed sentry has been with us from the time we came on board. This is just a precaution to cover all the options – do not take it personally.'

'What are we going to do from here on, professor?'

'Thank you, Tom, I was just getting to the plan that we now propose but before we do I would like Lily to fill you in on what October has been witnessing over these last days. Lily, please.' The professor waved at Lily and sat down in the rear row.

'What you are about to hear has been or will be briefed to all the teams that are in various places around the globe; the professor, Brian and I are your contact team from now on.'

'As you will know from my previous briefing in Wales – John's team was, of course, briefed separately in the south of England – we have been monitoring the anomalies by using the excellent data-gathering equipment on board October.' Lily flashed up a picture that had been taken as the Russian spacecraft was hit by the object that had been ejected from the anomaly.

'As you may remember, when the space vehicle was destroyed we assumed that the two cosmonauts aboard were killed. When David was returned we re-examined all the footage and telemetry from the spacecraft.' Another image came on next to the original picture.

'This is the medical information from the two crew members as the object impacted the spacecraft; the sequence of events is shown in milliseconds. You can see that the telemetry from the two ceased as the object contacted them. We have rerun this many times and we are now sure that the two were not aboard when it was destroyed but were removed, somehow, before contact.' Lily paused.

'Why do think all this is going on?' Oliver was now speaking. Joe was surprised that Oliver, or Billy, would ask questions because Joe thought that they already knew most of the answers – perhaps not.

'Oliver, please be reminded that our team here is only a fraction of the effort that is being expended on the problem so until we have gathered all the experiences of the teams we are unable to speculate on the end game. Remember, we initially thought that the Earth's gravitational field was being manipulated and that it was possible that it had occurred on Mars in the distant past. However, we have some more information that was gathered by the team working with October.'

Another image appeared on screen; it was of the anomaly out in space from which the cylinders had been coming. It was exactly the same as before: a seemingly two-dimensional object that could be viewed from in front and behind. The anomaly shimmered and faded but was always discernible against the background black of space.

Lily continued. 'This is a live feed from October. We have been observing this since the encounter with our spacecraft and one more cylinder appeared the day before yesterday; from its trajectory we thought it would land somewhere in East Africa but as it entered the lower atmosphere we lost it. It seems that it adopted the same method of hiding as the one in Wales. We have also been monitoring radiation output from the anomaly continuously since the ground operations began. As your teams entered the area there was a sharp increase in the output; why this was and what purpose it served is, as yet, unknown. But what we can now say for sure is that when things happen the radiation output from this point has increased; no radiation output, nothing happens. We have concluded that the radiation output on its own does not affect anything it is an indication that something is being manipulated; the radiation is a side effect if you like. One question was raised; if matter can be moved, removed and returned why are the cylinders being projected onto Earth from space? It was a good question but we do not know the answer; we need to determine what the cylinders are and what purpose they fulfil.'

'Thank you, Lily.' The professor was again on his feet.

'OK, where is all the stuff that is missing? As Lily has said we think that whatever is doing this can manipulate matter on a scale where they can disassemble anything and remake it later. How it is done is still a mystery. Obviously this is a technology way, way beyond anything that we can even dream about. Where did David go? We think that perhaps he didn't go anywhere, the dark room with moving walls was just what his consciousness experienced but he wasn't really there, in fact, he wasn't anywhere in the true sense. So we have a situation where large areas and objects are destroyed but with little or no debris and organic matter, in this case, David, can be removed and replaced. If we apply this thinking to the whole situation we have a sequence of events that removed things but did not destroy them. David, the two cosmonauts and Site A with all the people in it. Remember that David is convinced that whatever is doing this does not mean us harm. He was returned albeit slightly different. I can only think that anything that is alive is meant no harm. If that is the case what is it all about and what is happening here on Earth? Are we just connecting the state of Mars to Earth when there is no connection?

'I'm sorry to keep using the word "they"; it may be they or him or her or it but we don't know so "they" will do for now. Why all this is going on we can only speculate, so I won't.'

There was a rap on the door and the same commander came in with a file; he didn't say anything and avoided eye contact with everyone except the professor.

'Just arrived, professor,' the naval officer said handing the file over; he turned on his heel and left the room.

'Man of many words,' Billy said to his brother. The professor was leafing through the file quickly until he found the item he was looking for.

'Gentlemen, we have it; this information has come from our surveillance team in Ethiopia and it seems to confirm that we have located the last cylinder that came down the other day. It is now residing a couple of miles West of Asosa, a town near the Ethiopia–South Sudan border.'

'I have a really bad feeling about this,' Tom said under his breath to Joe as a map came on the screen. Joe shared Tom's thoughts; it was now seven years since the both of them had been in that area. They had worked a little further north from Asosa but still in the same bandit country; nice warm weather but not the place that would attract many tourists – not unless they fancy being on the nine o'clock news every night for a couple of weeks.

Joe looked around; he thought that perhaps half the assembled group had been out there, some more than once. He wondered if the Glaptons would turn out to have vast experience in the area. He made an odds-on bet with himself that they would.

The professor carried on. 'As you know the effort to gather information on this affair in general has been considerable; we here are only but a small part of the whole. Now we have located the last identified landing on Earth we can put plan B into operation, so to speak.'

The professor was trying to find something in his notes again. *He should get himself a tablet or some other device to manage it all,* Joe thought to himself.

'We now have three sites that contain an object that have been identified; so far we have not approached them or made any overt effort to determine what these three are doing; perhaps they are the same as the ones already encountered but we cannot be sure. Previously, as you all know, any attempt by us to deal with them has been met with either the objects disappearing or the object and other things around them disappearing. So now the organisation is in the waiting game. All we are doing is monitoring any output from the objects and trying to determine if it is having any effect on their surroundings.'

The professor rearranged his notes and put them down on the table. He had the remote in his hand and flicked through several images very quickly. 'Here we are; the first one that was located in Africa. Some of you may recall the talk given by Doctor Smyth the other day at Site A; well he showed us the old picture of an object that had been encountered on Mars by the Sojourner Rover. The object was dormant and had been there for quite some time. Gentlemen, we have found another one that is probably not as old as the Mars object but this time it is here in East Africa, not too far from the one that has just arrived.'

A map of the area appeared on screen showing the same area that had been talked about previously: a large scrub area in the region of Asosa. 'Again this object is, as far as we can tell, completely dormant. It was discovered by chance when we were looking for the most recent arrival. Odd, don't you think?'

The professor didn't wait for an answer but carried on.

'At this time we do not have many boots on the ground in this area but we do have substantial surveillance assets dedicated to monitoring it.'

The map disappeared and was replaced by an aerial photograph of a cliff side that ran away into the distance; it appeared that the drone was flying down a small valley with a river at the bottom, a steep cliff on one side and a slightly rising bank on the other that led out to farmland. The picture changed as the drone flew along the valley. The third picture was now on the screen.

'Let us just consider this image for a moment; if we change to false colour you will notice this object about halfway up the cliff.'

The colour changed and the image was zoomed in; a silver grey object was centre screen; the image cleared and a cylinder shape could be seen sticking out of the rock; it was lying in the direction of the valley so that one whole side was visible.

'Compared to the Mars object, we think this is a relative newcomer; only been there for around sixty-five million years. The rock was laid down from deposits on an ancient sea floor around the time most of the dinosaurs departed. What is it doing there? We know so little that about this and the Earth during this time we simply do not know.'

'How did we find it, professor?' Oliver was now taking an interest.

'If we had come this way a year ago we would have missed it; it was only exposed after half the cliff face fell into the river. Since we only found this by accident we expect there to be thousands of the things around the globe. We have an aerial vehicle that can mount a type P spectral analysis device. This allows us to monitor output from just about anything, including the ground. This object is completely dormant; no output at all whilst the rock in which it sits does produce some very low-level radiation. So we noticed it because it was so quiet. Since we can see it, it obviously reflects light in the visible wavelength but that is all. As previously mentioned we were looking for the latest arrival but found this first. The more recent one is a couple of miles further down the rift and on the valley floor. We cannot see it though; it seems to be hiding, as was the one in the Welsh valley.'

Billy held his hand up. 'Yes, Billy, you have a question?'

'What are the rest of teams doing about this; have we people in other areas? If we have what is the aim of the complete operation at this time?

'As you know already there are other teams out in the area but since we have had at least one team member compromised by whatever we are facing we must assume that there are or will be others that are compromised in a similar way. Remember that David came back to us with some knowledge of what we were doing and that he felt that whatever was doing this didn't mean us any direct harm. We must assume that knowledge is or has been transferred in both directions; so anything David knew is now known by the other side. To that end we will only concern ourselves with the detail of what we personally will be engaged in. No more information regarding what the other teams and agencies are doing will be discussed unless it has a direct bearing on what we here are going to be doing. If we don't have the information then we cannot give it away either intentionally or unintentionally. Before you ask, I or anybody here does not know the full picture.'

'So to continue, we know there are two objects in the area of concern but there may be more. One of the known objects, as far as we can tell, is old and now completely dormant the other is active and trying not to be found.'

Brian was back at the front standing next to the professor. 'Gentlemen I will now let Brian talk you through one of the items that has been brought to our attention since we started to look in this area of Ethiopia, Brian.'

The screen changed to show an image that some of them recognised; it showed a single-storey building with high windows and appeared to be religious in style; probably not that large and had a square or almost square floor plan.

'The Ark of the Covenant!' Tom was now speaking, not quite believing where this could be going.

Brian smiled. 'Yes, indeed or, to be precise, the place where the Ark is supposed to be.'

'Let me fill you all in with a little history lesson; the Ark was constructed around three thousand years ago in order to contain the stone tablets that listed the Ten Commandments given to Moses by the Almighty. If the historical records can be believed the Ark was kept in King Solomon's Temple in

Jerusalem until the Babylonians occupied the area in about the sixth century BC. It is at this time the trail gets a little muddled with the Ark supposedly being places such as southern France, England and even the USA. However, the most consistently mentioned location is a small town in Northern Ethiopia called Aksum; the spelling varies from account to account.

'The town, however, does exist, hence this rather recent photograph. If the Ark is in Ethiopia it has moved several times since its arrival; this building was built on the direction of the Emperor Haile Selassie and was dedicated by him in the sixties. Before it was put into this place the Ark was in the Mary of Zion Church, which is very close to the current building. The town of Aksum is about a thousand kilometres, as the crow flies, from Asosa and our current interest.'

Joe's mind was now racing: *Mars! Moving rock formations! And now the Ark of the Covenant! It gets better all the time.* He thought that it must make sense to someone because it didn't to him.

'Lily and her team from October have been correlating the magnetic-field changes since we started on the enterprise so I will let her tell you what has been found regarding this area.'

Brain sat down as Lily stood up.

'Remember when we thought that the Earth's magnetic field was being modified somehow by the output from the objects we have encountered? Well, we were not totally correct in assuming what we did; the field has been changing but we now think that it is not being driven by the objects.' She pressed the remote and a graph appeared on screen; it was an illustration of the Earth's magnetic field with a number one at the top.

'Slide one as you can see shows the normal arrangement we expect to find if there were little or no solar activity out of the ordinary.'

The picture changed to show a similar view of the Earth with the field overlaid. This time the field was distorted in several places, one being the Northern Ethiopia area; the lines seemed to converge and then return to the symmetrical. On the African continent there appeared to be at least five definite areas that were changed.

'As you can see the area we are interested in shows a distortion of the field that we would not normally expect – remember, at this time there is no unusual solar activity to account for what we see.'

Slide three came on the screen; it was a closer, more detailed view of the north-east of Africa. There were two distinct areas of distortion, one bigger than the other.

'The large, strong one is over the object that fell to Earth recently – the one we have been looking for since it arrived. The other, weaker one is directly over the town of Aksum. When we found this we went back a number of years and looked at the magnetic field date for this area; what we found was surprising. This distortion over Aksum has been here since we started recording the data. Interesting, don't you think?'

'Why has this not been noticed before, Lily? Billy was asking the obvious question.

'Because we weren't looking for it. Any chance observation would have been put down to variations in the field due to the Sun's activity. It only became obvious because we were looking for the recent arrival. It is, however, somewhat different from all the other field changes; it remains constant whereas all the rest change when something is going on. All the closest ones to your little adventure in Wales underwent several changes before returning to a background level. We have looked at all the other changes and compared the timeframe to this one; it is unchanged and does not change at all.'

'Why all the stuff in Wales and Cornwall then?' Tom asked.

'I wondered when someone would get to that,' Lily said changing the image to another graph, a linear one with peaks and troughs.

'If you look at the timeline for this record of magnetic changes you will notice that whilst your teams were experiencing the movements in the cave system the overall magnetic field was fluctuating quite considerably; but not the field in and around Aksum, however.' The slide changed and she pointed to Aksum.

'Getting back to your question about why all the odd stuff; we think that there was nothing to be found in either Wales or Cornwall and of course all the other sites that have been investigated. We have, we believe, been led on a "wild goose chase" as some of you say; all of the "stuff" going on was a distraction. Good news, no?'

'Why so?'

'Because, my dear Oliver, we obviously need to be distracted from what is really going on. On the plus side we are certainly a threat because if we were not we could be totally ignored; one thing is for sure, we are not being ignored. The only thing to answer now is what *is* going on?'

The watchers were planning to move along with the schedule; in twenty rotations the second phase would begin. So far the interference of the individuals had not delayed anything. Quite the contrary, in fact, most of what had been planned had gone unnoticed because the deception had worked well. It was thought that perhaps the level of intelligence and capability had been overestimated but time would tell. The first individual taken had been returned but there had been some unforeseen problems with the return. It had been necessary to modify it so that it would assemble correctly; the change in makeup was now known so that error would not happen again should a return be repeated.

'So we think that the item that might be the Ark of the Covenant in Aksum is playing a part in the magnetic variations that are going on?' Tom asked the question for the rest of them.

'Yes and no,' Lily began. 'We now have a lot more data on the magnetic changes than we had when you were deployed in the valley and the caves; but if you look at this.' The picture changed to another graph this time in multicolour. 'Just to confirm what I have been saying, please look at this. You will see that by comparing the timeline and the changes, the output in Aksum didn't change at all whilst every other one did whilst you and the other teams were operating.' The graph did show that every time the teams entered or were in the cave systems the output from some areas changed considerably but the area around Aksum just showed the same reading as every time before. 'So the item in Aksum is playing some sort of part but it doesn't seem to be involved in the run-around you all had.'

'So where do we go from here?'

'We go to Ethiopia or at least some of us will go to Ethiopia – more on that when the military element briefs us tomorrow. Yes, gentlemen, we are all now under military control; in our case this little group now reports to the United States Navy, who in turn are under command of the central committee that has been set up at the UN.' Lily was smiling.

'Under command of the UN, now there's a thing,' Joe said under his breath.

The professor was now at the front standing next to Lily. 'Gentlemen, that concludes today's session. I will just end here by saying that things are moving along at a pace and that we will be conducting an operation in Ethiopia when we are in a position to put you ashore. As Lily has said, more to follow when the United States Navy brief us tomorrow. I'm sorry I cannot be more exact but I don't want to steal anyone's thunder. Have a good night's rest and we will be in here again at 0700.'

18.

The aircraft carrier was now in the Mediterranean having passed through the Straits of Gibraltar the evening before; the USS *Ronald Reagan* was pushing thirty-five knots and had been for most of the journey from the west coast of Ireland. It was not alone, of course, the whole carrier group was tagging along; at the moment thousands of sailors were under the command of a fleet admiral with the sole task of delivering a handful of men to the drop off point.

In a few days it would pass through the Suez Canal and then transit the Red Sea to be off the coast of Eritrea and at the southern end of the Red Sea; easily within striking distance of the area of concern in Ethiopia. All sorts of diplomatic negotiations had been going on in the background; there was a not an inconsiderable lobby that was trying to stop the carrier force from going this way. Arguments ranging from the proximity of the force close to the holy city of Mecca to the fear that the local tribes in that region would see the arrival of a large American aircraft carrier as the start of an invasion that would upset the delicate balance of power in the respective areas of interest. For now it looked like the force would be in position without any undue delay.

Bright and early the two teams assembled in the conference room to await the arrival of the US Navy team that was to brief them for the next phase, whatever that turned out to be.

A tall, very lean officer came into the room and strode to the front.

'Good morning, gentlemen, I am Colonel Johnson, United States Marine Corps. I will be your guide from now on until this operation can be concluded in a satisfactory manner. I have been briefed on all your backgrounds and experience up to this point. If there are any questions or if there is anyone who does not wish to continue, please speak now.'

The colonel's gaze swept the room holding each and all the seated men for a half a second or so. No one said anything; each, like Joe, thought that it would become clear when the briefing started. None of the men in the room felt like leaving the operation at this point.

'Would the following men stay here: Billy, Joe, Tom and Oliver. The rest will be briefed separately. Remember what the professor said about the chances of being compromised; all information passed from now on will be on a need to know basis; suffice it to say, both your teams will be in support of each other but you will be trained and briefed separately. OK, on you go.'

The men not mentioned by name got up and left; John Flett raised an eyebrow to Joe as he went past. The colonel waited for the group to leave the room and the door to close behind them.

'OK, gentlemen from here on we are going to become the best of friends; we will be spending a lot of time together so I will give you another chance to leave.' There was silence in the room with no one making any sound.

'As I thought; we will be a good team.'

An image appeared on the screen; it was a detailed map of the area around Asosa in Ethiopia that they had been shown by Lily a couple of days before. Perhaps it was weeks before; the four men were becoming a little confused and bemused by what had been thrown at them so far. There had been lots of information but no real direction as to what was going to be expected of them from now on.

'You have all seen this map before, of course. The information on it remains the same except for the detail that I will now impart to you.'

The image zoomed in to the town of Asosa; close enough to determine the street and building pattern. The image moved over so that only the western edge of the town was visible. One building was highlighted in red, the rest all remained in a dull brown colour.

'This is where we are going in a couple of days from now. I said we but I mean you; a four-man team with a specific objective, what that objective is will become clear as we train for insertion. Be aware that this operation is backed at the highest level; there can be no room for failure from any of us.'

'What exactly are we to do in this little red building, colonel?' Tom had his hand up but he only just got to the question before the other three.

'Remember one of the objects was tracked from the anomaly and entered the atmosphere before ending up outside Asosa; at this time we discovered the old one in the valley side. Well, gentlemen, the one that "fell to Earth" has not remained where it fell; it is now, we think, in or under the red house. How it moved and why is not a total mystery but it is displaying characteristics that the others did not. You four are going to go and try and retrieve it.'

Joe raised his hand. We tried to do things to these objects before but failed miserably, what makes you think we can simply go and retrieve it; even nuclear weapons failed to budge them before.'

'Thanks for that, Joe.' *We haven't been introduced but he knows my name; maybe it was a one-in-four guess,* Joe thought.

'We think that the four of you can retrieve this one because how it got from the landing site to where it is now is known.' Another image appeared on screen. It was obviously taken from some sort of surveillance asset, probably a drone but could have been a high-altitude aircraft that was passing. It showed a pickup truck, a technical in local parlance; on the back of it was the cylinder-like object that they had all seen examples of before.

'The man driving the truck was seen simply picking this thing up; he didn't have any help that we could see and the object did not appear to be heavy. He simply drove up to it and loaded it into the back. As you know this object was invisible when it arrived; we only discovered it by the differences in magnetic field but now it is visible and being transported in the back of a local truck! How is this?'

'The object is malfunctioning or has become dormant, a bit like the very old ones that we have encountered on Mars and in the side of the valley.' Billy was guessing, of course, but it seemed a logical explanation. One thing that was worrying is that if it had failed it must be some sort of device or machine.

'Exactly what the team thought when the guy just went to it with his truck and picked it up. It is likely that he is just an opportunist and doesn't know what it is or what he wants it for. Remember, there are many very poor people in this area and, if that isn't enough, the population are plagued by bandits following one despot or another. It is probably because it is shiny and might be of use some time in the future – an idea that most soldiers in most armies can relate to.'

The image changed to the moment that the man picked the object up. 'As you can see the guy had no problems lifting this into the back of the vehicle, even an empty forty-gallon oil drum would have been awkward but this seems to be as light as a feather.'

The picture changed and sure enough the man appeared to be holding the object off the ground with one hand while he undid the rear of the vehicle.

'Why don't we just go in mob-handed and get this thing? A large force, simply swamp the area and take it away.' Tom was being practical now, surely there was no need to be covert in this: just go and get it.

'Yes, Tom, we could do that but we still have a little control over who and what organisations know about what we are doing. If we turn up with a task force and start landing a couple of hundred people on the ground it will soon be world news and everybody and his uncle will know we are there. By using a small team we can carry this out without too much drama. There is also the option of deniability if things go belly up. As you know there are and have been for some time small groups of outside contractors in this area, doing all manner of jobs from pure mercenary to close protection and the like. If we fail or are compromised whilst in the area it would be easy to explain our presence as personnel of a private security firm doing heaven knows what.'

Both Tom and Joe had been in similar situations around the world; get in quick, get out quick and if you are caught we will help if we can but not if it compromises the organisation. The money is good though.

'Are there any more questions before we get to business?' The colonel had expected a lot more discussion than this but he had worked with Brits before and they could usually be relied upon to do the job with only minor questioning, unlike some other agencies he had worked with and one in particular that he had just set off on a task the day before.

None of the four raised a hand and all were looking directly at the colonel. 'Outstanding!'

'Today is day one of a fourteen-day operation; if it looks like it will extend beyond the fourteen days it will likely be stopped and cancelled. The reason for the time constraint is that there are other agencies at work; I remind you again that you are not alone in this endeavour, although it may seem like it at times from now on in.'

The colonel handed each man a folder, which contained several pages of typed information and several photographs. 'These folders and the information contained in them are not to leave this room. You may read and discuss the information contained but leave them here when you leave. From now on this room will be the planning room for the next phase. We will now have a bite to eat and continue in the afternoon; the food will be here shortly.'

As the colonel stopped speaking the door opened and several US Navy personnel came in carrying trays of food and placed it all on the low table that were along one wall. A box with cutlery and condiments came with it. The Navy people didn't say anything or make eye contact and left immediately once they had put the food down. Either the colonel was psychic or he was following a strict timetable.

'Let's eat, gentlemen.' The colonel had already picked up a plate.

All the way through the meal the five men chatted about previous experiences that they had all been involved in; it came as a surprise how knowledgeable the colonel was of the four's past history; he was obviously well briefed.

The meal lasted about half an hour, by which time the five had all they wanted to eat and right on cue the Navy personnel returned to carry away all the used crockery and any waste that had been generated. The tea and coffee was refilled and the Navy left, again without a word.

'Please be seated, gentlemen, we will carry on with the

briefing that will set us on the way to the conclusion of this operation. So far we have discussed the location of the object and the fact that it is fairly close to where it came down. We know that for some reason it has been moved by a local after it became visible. Why and how all this happened is not our concern at the moment. In about five days we will be in a position to insert you four into the area of interest. When you are there your task is to secure the object so that it can be retrieved and relocated here on board the *Ronald Reagan*. Once the object is here your job will be done.' The colonel paused and seemed to think about what he was going to say.

'The four of you have been chosen specifically for this task because you are, without doubt, the best we have available. So far the four of you have performed exactly as expected and we are sure you are the right team for this undertaking. Are there any questions?'

Oliver put up his hand. 'If we are to be inserted into that area, we will need to get a bit of sunshine to acclimatise to the change in humidity and temperature. We will also need some training and rehearsal for this job. Also, how will the object and this team be withdrawn from the area once we have secured the target?'

'Yes to all of that; we have a training regime in place that you will take part in over the following days; you will spend all day on deck and only get away from the weather when you are sleeping. From when you leave this room you will have no access to any air-conditioning of any sort. Once we have finished this brief you are as if you have been deployed.'

'Looking forward to it, colonel.' Billy was ready to go.

'In a moment your training team leaders will report here and take you to the kit store so that any equipment you need can be provided; over the next few days you are perfectly at liberty to discard or modify the kit that you have. Do not concern yourself with the expense or worry that you have changed the gear several times only to return to the original.'

Over the following couple of days the team did indeed modify and discard equipment. They also slept out on deck and spent long days in the open out on the flight deck. The whole carrier seemed to be at their disposal with very little coming or going of aircraft; in fact, the only aircraft they saw the whole time were some Blackhawks that arrived and immediately left once they had discharged their cargo – quite something for a vessel that could conduct major air operations as matter of routine. Of course, the rest of the carrier group could be seen from time to time, several air defence vessels and other ships that escorted the *Ronald Reagan* wherever it went. The carrier was far too valuable an asset to let it out on its own.

At the end of the third day they started training in the complexities of mounting and dismounting from the Blackhawk. They were under direction of a very large marine called Spike – what his real name was they never found out. He was one serious marine who didn't seem to get tired of the job – ever! Under his instruction they practised getting on and off the aircraft until they could do it in the dark; at one stage he even had them wear a full-head helmet that prevented them from seeing anything at all. It is amazing what you can learn to do if driven hard enough. All four came to the obvious conclusion that the operation would be at night with perhaps one day of lying up somewhere in the open countryside. Time would tell. The training continued with descents from about fifty metres to the ship's deck, with and without loads.

On the last day before deployment the training took another turn; a new man was part of the training team, this time a civilian. They were back in the conference room for a couple of hours going over some new equipment that they would all carry.

The new addition was James Dolan who spoke with a distinctive Welsh accent. The group wondered how he was Welsh with a name like that; Oliver did ask him but James ignored the question as if he hadn't heard it.

'OK, I am here to show you one or two things that might make your journey a little easier. Firstly, this device, which you will all wear on your right arm, is a much-improved version of the device that Oliver was wearing when you went into the caves in Ireland. It will generate a magnetic field of an intensity that will effectively screen you from the field that we think the objects are putting out. Remember that we do not fully understand the objects purpose but Oliver did manage to hide the group to some extent.'

The device that was shown was indeed similar to the one that Oliver had activated in Ireland but was a little bigger but still not so big as to get in the way; it had an on-switch and three small lights with only one on at any time.

James began explaining the device. 'This can be slipped over the hand and adjusted with this pull strap to make it fit comfortably. The on/off switch is a simple push to "on" and another push to "off"; it is recessed so you shouldn't be able to operate it simply by rubbing against anything by accident. The first of the three lights shows when the device is on; it will flicker when the battery power is reaching a critical level. The middle light will illuminate should an exterior magnetic influence be detected; we know that the objects do transmit X-rays but they also seem to affect the ambient electromagnetic field that is in the area. Lastly a new addition: this one will illuminate should you be displaced as you were in Ireland; it if comes on you are to evacuate, if you can, immediately. We know some of this stuff works from the time Oliver was using a similar device but we cannot be one hundred per cent certain.'

They all took the device, fitting it to their right arms and adjusted the strapping that held it in place.

'The battery should last for at least seven days but may last longer depending on how the lights behave; there is no audible warning so you need to keep a eye on it.'

James let them have a minute for trial and error in the fitment; once they were all happy he continued.

'This item is new and you will have not seen it before.' He put a similarly shaped device as the electromagnetic item onto the table; this time it was about twice the size and, judging by the way he handled it Joe thought it was considerably heavier.

'This will give you an advantage if you come up against it. You will remember that every time we have deployed an Electrical Discharge Weapon the object has disappeared; we do not know if the objects were destroyed or they simply moved to somewhere else. The EDW does, however, give us a get-out should we – or rather you – need it. The power comes from a small unit that will be worn on your back; it will give enough juice to get two maybe three discharges from the device. The output is considerable but not as much as the much larger weapon we deployed in Wales. Joe, please be the first to try a fit.' James offered the device to Joe who held his arm out to be fitted.

Joe waved his arm around in an arc to get the feel.

'Remember that it will be connected to the power supply on your back.'

'Seems fine and not all that clumsy; how much does the power supply weigh?' Joe asked.

'Fifteen kilograms plus around one kilogram for the connection and harness.'

All four tried on the device while James made sure the fit was right.

'How is it fired?' Tom said.

'There is a trigger device that sits in the palm of your hand; by squeezing your fingers together and aiming your hand at the target the discharge will be released. You will still be able to fire a conventional weapon from this hand without triggering the EDW. Neither the power pack nor the trigger device is in this room. Later we will have an opportunity to test fire it but be assured it is not the sort of thing to discharge in a space like this.'

'All the other kit you will be carrying you are already familiar with; these two items are at the top of the restricted list so please do not lose them. We will now let you have a feel for these devices out on the fantail please leave the units on, you will be wearing them for some time from now.'

The four were led out of the briefing room and up onto the flight deck; once there they walked to the stern of the carrier. It was getting light and the heat was already in the high twenties. The set-up on the flight deck was a large object that seemed to have been grown from the very steel of the ship.

'Gentlemen, this is the catcher that you will each aim your weapon at. We will do it one at a time so that you can practice in slow time and we can make any adjustments that are needed. Now these crewmen will put your battery pack on and set up the trigger device one at a time. Because this weapon is extremely capable only one device at a time will be set to go.'

The four were marshalled into a line opposite the structure.

'Joe, you can be first.'

Joe stepped forward and was helped with putting the battery onto his back; it wasn't as heavy as he imagined it would be and was quite comfortable. There would be no problems carrying this for a couple of hours at least. A navy technician then connected the trigger device after attaching it to Joe's hand.

'Right, Joe, I would like you to point with your thumb at the catcher and squeeze the trigger in the palm of your hand.'

Joe raised his hand as if pointing his thumb at the target; with a slight squeeze the weapon discharged. The flash came as a surprise to Joe; a massive flash and an arc of electrical discharge leaped at the target. The image only lasted for half a second but all four of the team were more than impressed. The air was full of the smell from the discharge.

'Alright, Joe?' The colonel was smiling.

'Wow! That was something else.' Joe was very impressed with the new weapon.

All four men took it in turns to test the new weapon; the whole process being under very tight control with the device being powered down and the battery disconnected after each firing by the technician from the carrier crew. After a few hours of firing and adjusting the four men felt competent in the operation of the EDW.

'Gentlemen.' The colonel waved the four into a group so that he could be heard; the other crew and James left the immediate area so that they were not in earshot.

'We are now good to go and will be into the insertion launch area in about twelve hours. As you will appreciate there has to be a command structure within any team. Joe, you are in command. Tom, you are second in command. Oliver, you are third in line and, Billy, if it gets down to only one you are in charge.' The four men realised that this was a fairly notional pecking order. The only thing that mattered was the job in hand; they would all work as one: get the job done then go home.

'Hey, Billy, I'm your boss, that makes a change doesn't it.' Billy was not at all worried at the pecking order, he had the utmost confidence in his brother and either of them would follow the other no matter what. As far as Joe and Tom were concerned both Oliver and Billy were well aware of their credentials and had no worries about their ability. The team was a good one.

19.

The four men were now over the Red Sea approaching the coast of Eritrea. Joe had done the sums in his head when they were told to route into Asosa in North Western Ethiopia; he reckoned that they could get there but the Blackhawk wouldn't have enough fuel to get back to the carrier. No big deal he had been dropped from a chopper at the extreme limit of range many times; the journey would take the helicopter on to a refuelling point or would be refuelled in mid-air but that would be risky because the whole operation would be detected by any local who were using radar such as air-traffic control at the several airports and landing strips they would transit over. The range problem of the helicopter was not his so he put it out of his mind and thought about what they would do when they were delivered. At this rate of travel it would be several hours before they were in place. The other three team members were asleep, making the most of the time available as it was uncertain if they would have much rest time once on the ground.

The watchers were monitoring the progress of the helicopter and were making plans to deal with it if it became a threat.

'Why are they going to this place?' one asked.

'Unknown, but it is believed that they are to make contact with the unit that has been moved.'

'Shall we intervene?'

'No, not at this time.'

Joe was now asleep as the helicopter dropped down to about fifty feet above the ground; it was showing no lights and was taking an indirect route to avoid hazards such as power lines and communication towers that had been identified in the days prior to launch. The two pilots were very experienced in this sort of thing and were confident that all would go to plan; almost a routine job that they had done many times before. Insertion point would be in four and a half hours; then across the border to refuel and some rest before going on call for extraction. Somewhere out to the north was the second aircraft but that was not there concern at the moment.

The pilot slowed the forward momentum of the helicopter before turning into the wind and landing in a clearing amongst some low trees and scrub, typical countryside for this part of the world. The landing point had been selected from at least a dozen that would have been adequate for the job. Only a short time on the ground and then they would be on their way.

The four-man team were ready immediately as the chopper touched down; with a friendly wave to the two crewmen, the team exited the aircraft and ran into the cover of the nearby trees. The Blackhawk lifted off and was gone, only a receding noise to indicate it had ever been there.

It was just after two in the morning when Joe looked at his watch. 'We are here, about half a click from the house that is of interest. We should be able to get there before three if we don't encounter anyone.'

Joe made the sign for silence then put his hand in the air and made the sign for the team to follow. All four knew the drill so all fell in line, spacing themselves out so as to be able to give cover to the man in front but not so close as to be compromised by anyone seeing the man in front. Stay apart but stay in support of each other.

The going was fairly easy and the temperature was quite pleasant; during the day when the sun was at its highest this would change, hopefully by then they would be out of here and on their way back.

The first house, if that was what it was, came into view: a single-story structure with a doorway and a single window on the side they could see. Joe stopped and indicated that Oliver should get a little closer to determine what if anything was about. Oliver trotted off and disappeared around the side of the building. Moments later he appeared at the opposite side having gone all the way round.

'A small house with at least one person inside – snoring like a train.' He was right next to Joe so that he didn't need to raise his voice above a whisper.

'Excellent and so far no dogs, but there are bound to be some on the way in.'

Just as Joe had spoken a dog started to bark but it was some way off on the right, not on the route in it so shouldn't bother them. Another dog joined in but it was close to the first. They moved off and very soon came to a dirt road; it showed signs of heavy use but that was not unusual for this part of the world and certainly normal for this edge-of-town area. The house grouping was now tighter with one even showing a light. Joe gave the signal to stop and sent Oliver out to see what significance the light had.

'Nothing happening in there; I think they left the light on or they leave it on at night: nothing stirring and all quiet.'

They were being watched, however: a very large mastiff-type dog that was showing the scars of many a fight. Its owner, Jamal, who was asleep in the house with the light, had acquired the dog some time ago and was very proud in the way he had trained it; no barking but a very vicious and brave dog. He was excellent for guarding his property and had taken many a thief completely by surprise, it had even killed a man who had once tried to steal grain from his store at the side of the house. He had called the dog George after the American president; a very funny name, he thought, and it often amused him that George was a dog.

As Tom passed, the dog launched itself into him; Oliver saw it first but was not quick enough to warn anyone. The dog was onto Tom and sank its teeth into the EDW control that was on his arm. Tom was brought down immediately; the dog was very powerful and was probably close to Tom's weight. Oliver was on them in a second; the dog gave a single whimper than was silent. Oliver replaced his combat knife and moved the dog from on top of Tom. The dog was dead with the knife thrust going through the third and fourth vertebrae.

'Thanks for that.' Tom was impressed at Oliver's skill in dealing with the dog and was very glad he was on hand to do it.

'Any injuries?' Joe was examining Tom's arm. 'No, this little device saved my bacon this time but I think that it won't work from now on.' The warning device on Tom's arm had been torn apart by the dog but it had not damaged his arm to any extent. Quite a bit of bruising but he would survive.

'OK, get this thing out of the way. The good thing here is that there were no injuries and the dog didn't alert anyone; strange it didn't bark. Let's keep our eyes peeled for anything similar from now on.'

Billy and Oliver dragged the dog into some low scrub that was across the road. It would be hidden for now but not once the sun came up and the other occupants of the town were up and about. There was very little blood from the wound in the dog's neck; if the knife had gone into an artery or a lung there would be blood all over the place and difficult to clean up effectively. Tom was still surprised at the skill Oliver had displayed – impressive.

Joe indicated that Billy should lead for the next leg; they could soon be in the area where the object was thought to be. Joe assumed that all would go to plan and they could recover the object to the pickup point on the outskirts. It all depended on how manageable the object was; it seemed to be very light and could easily be carried by one man, as they had seen in the drone footage. That's if the man who was seen picking it up did not have super-human strength.

The next ten minutes went without incident and they were soon outside the target house; it was single-story building but was a little bigger than the ones that surrounded it. There were two satellite dishes on the roof pointing in different directions.

'Seems they like to watch a lot of television,' Billy said, pointing at the roof.

Joe indicated that they should all switch on their electro-magnetic countermeasure devices, at the same time switching his own on. The power light came on and immediately dimmed to account for the dark. The other two lights remained off.

'So far so good,' remarked Joe. 'Billy, take a look around the house and see if you can locate the object; hopefully it is not in the owner's bedroom under his bed. Tom and Oliver, you place yourselves to give cover should we need it; Billy and me will go and get the object.'

Joe, send a burst message from his Pinger, with any luck they would be out of here with the object and at the rendezvous before the pickup chopper arrived. They would be cutting it fine but there was no choice.

Billy came back with a smile on his face. 'We are in luck. The object is under a lean-to at the back of the house; we won't need to wake the owner up and ask for it.'

'OK, let's go; if we are compromised we all break up and meet at the extraction point. Remember, the chopper will not wait and it is a very long walk home.'

Joe and Billy moved forward to the edge of the house and disappeared round the corner. In no time at all they reappeared carrying the object; it did seem to be made of some sort of shiny material but appeared to weigh nothing at all; the two men were moving at speed and didn't seem to have any problems with the objects size or weight. They presented a rather ridiculous sight.

Joe and Billy didn't pause but ran straight past the other two and continued out towards the extraction point about a kilometre away. At this rate they should make the chopper without any problems. The object was moved at best speed whilst Tom and Oliver followed continually checking for any signs of pursuit. They stopped several times to listen for any more from the edge of town. There was nothing; it all seemed to be going to plan.

They reached the pickup point without incident; it would still be a couple of hours before the sun rose. All four men were gathered round the object wondering at the lightness of it. It was possible to pick it up with one finger if it was balanced on one end – quite remarkable.

'The lift should be here anytime now so let's get the perimeter secured and be ready to go.' Joe was now looking at his Pinger, which had sounded.

'Inbound, three minutes,' Joe announced.

The helicopter could now be heard, very faintly off to the west; within moments the aircraft could be seen coming in low of the stinted trees that covered the land from the edge of town to the horizon. A cloud of dust and the helicopter was with them, settling down in the open area. The men wasted no time and pushed the object into the cargo area and strapping it down with a single ratchet strap that held it in the mid position. The four men boarded and sat in the seats that were either side of their new cargo. In a cloud of dust, the helicopter launched into the sky, turned and headed east.

As the helicopter cleared some low trees an alarm sounding in the cockpit: a beep, beep that couldn't be ignored.

'We have problem!' The pilot said over the intercom.

'What is it? Do we need to abort?' Joe was talking into the microphone that was attached to the headset they were all wearing.

'Losing lift at an alarming rate; we should get on deck and have a look.' The pilot made a turn and set the helicopter down; the alarm ceased and all seemed well: the rotor was still turning and there were no unusual sounds from the engine and gearbox that was over their heads.

The pilot explained to the team what had happened. 'As we got to fifty feet we lost lift, not because of any malfunction that we could determine but it was as if we had taken a load that was beyond the lift capabilities of the aircraft. Shouldn't have happened – these babies can lift ten times the weight we have at the moment. All seems fine now though. We will do a couple of checks and then we should be on our way.'

The two pilots went through a fairly comprehensive checklist and came up with nothing; everything was operating as expected: there were no errors, not even minor ones. The Blackhawk was behaving as it should, at least whilst on the ground.

The pilot changed the pitch to give maximum lift for a quick climb and getaway. The helicopter seemed to judder but remained on the ground. It was at this point that Tom noticed something.

'Abort take off!' Tom said into the microphone as calmly as he could.

The engine tone subsided and the lift was taken off.

'Take a look at this.' The pilot came into the rear cabin and looked at a point on the floor that Tom had indicated. There was damage where the object touched the floor of the helicopter, as if the object was suddenly very heavy; it had pushed itself into the floor by a couple of centimetres. Tom loosened the strap that was over and gave the object a push; it moved very easily and bounced of Oliver's legs. Under where the object had been there was a definite depression in the floor.

'I've seen something similar before but that was caused by a very heavy landing with cargo that was at the maximum weight.' The co-pilot was offering some experience but it didn't explain this. The landing was not hard and they were now unable to even take off; yet the object seemed to have the mass of a large piece of polystyrene that could be pushed around with little effort.

Joe was entering something into his Pinger. The response was very quick.

'We are to leave the object here and evacuate without it; ditch the thing outside and we can go.'

All four of the team cleared the restraining strap out of the way and began to push the object out of the door; it didn't move and acted like it was stuck to the floor. No matter how much effort they applied it would not move towards the door. It was possible to move it around the inside of the aircraft, however.

'It looks like it doesn't want to leave and doesn't like flying.' They were all a little baffled.

Oliver was looking at the warning device he had on his arm; the middle light was on indicating a magnetic field was in play.

'We have a fairly large field being generated here; I think that it is causing the object to increase in mass. How it does that I have no idea. Our arm units should mask our presence but if we put our arms out over the object perhaps we can hide it from the field.' He held his arms and held the hands of the people opposite and next to him; a loose circle was formed over the object.

'OK, let's try again,' Oliver said to the pilot.

The engine pitch changed as the angle of the rotor changed to give more lift; the helicopter climbed away from the ground without the previous problem.

'Looks like we will be holding hands for the journey back, fellas.'

The helicopter headed east into the dawn. Joe was thinking what might happen when they landed on the deck of the carrier; should be interesting at the very least.

On the way back there were several worrying episodes when the team relaxed their grip on each other or moved their arms to relieve the fatigue. Each time this happened, the alarm on the flight deck would trigger and only stop when the position of the linked arms was adjusted.

'Get on the blower and tell the colonel and the professor that we need an electromagnetic containment set-up on deck ready for when we land.' Oliver was speaking to the pilot hoping that none of the power supplies would fail before they got there; it would be a long walk – or swim – home.

Five minutes later the helicopter gave a very violent lurch to the right; all manner of alarms sounded on the control panel and the aircraft plummeted towards the ground. The engines screamed as the pilot tried to get more lift. Just as it seemed that they would pile into the ground the helicopter levelled out and landed. The pilot began the close down procedure as fast as he and the co-pilot could manage.

'That was one scary moment!' The co-pilot spoke for everyone.

'What happened there? Was it something wrong with the aircraft or what?' Joe was talking to the two flight crew who were now going through a checklist.

'Not the aircraft; it felt as if we were in a sudden gust of crosswind at hurricane force. We were not of course; wind speed is about half a click from the south – nothing that could affect us.

'Have a look at this!' Billy was examining the point where the object was resting on the floor; it had pushed the floor in by a good two inches but the object was now as light as a feather again and could easily be moved by nudging it with his toe.

'Let's see if we can get it off and on to the ground; we can then leave it here and go. This thing is becoming a severe liability.'

Joe and Billy exited the helicopter and began to pull the object out of the door; Oliver and Tom pushed from inside. This time the object didn't resist at all and was on the ground in no time; whatever prevented them from moving it before didn't seem to be at work this time.

'No magnetic field in play now.' Oliver was looking at the device on his arm; the middle light was off. All four of the team were now looking for the tell-tale illumination on their arms: nothing was showing.

'What are we going to do now?' The pilot was talking to Joe.

'We have to get out of here or we will be having an audience before too long; the town is now waking up and I expect that we won't be welcomed with open arms. Tom, Billy and Oliver will get on the chopper and leave; I want you to loiter about a click away and then come back and get me if I'm still here. I will attempt to deal with the object with the EDW, if it works like the previous times we have used it the object will be destroyed; only problem is that on at least one occasion half the hill will go with it. If that happens don't bother coming back for me as I will not be here.

There was no argument or conversation from the group; they were all professional and accepted the plan at face value. There would be no leadership by committee.

The pilot had the turbines running as the three got onto the helicopter; the rotors started to turn and were soon up to full speed. The aircraft drove up a cloud of dust as it soured into the air; pitched lightly to the right and was gone.

Joe was stood by the object, running his hand over the smooth surface. 'What are you?'

Joe turned and walked away in the direction the helicopter had gone; at thirty paces he turned and checked the ready light on the weapon.

'Here goes nothing,' Joe said, not at all certain that he would be on this Earth for very much longer.

He pointed his thumb at the device just like he had practiced on the carrier and squeezed his fingers into the palm of his hand. *Strange weapon, this: no recoil but a blinding flash of light and the smell of electrical burning. Nice toy!* Joe thought.

The discharge arced away from Joe's arm and connected with the object; for a couple of seconds nothing seemed to happen then there was blinding flash of light, the likes of which Joe had never encountered before. The control device on Joe's arm burst into a hundred pieces and, at the same time, battery on his back seemed became hot then fell to bits. Joe was blinded by the intense light that had been generated and could only see stars dancing in front of his eyes. It was a couple of minutes before he could see anything except the image of the device.

Joe removed the remnants of the battery and harness from his back; he gathered up all the pieces he could find and put them into a stuff sack that he had in a pocket; no sense in leaving anything behind. Joe walked over to where the object had been; there was no trace at all of it, not even a mark on the ground.

The Blackhawk returned and did a low pass over the area; the pilot saw Joe and came into land blowing up a cloud of dust that obscured everything. In an instant, Joe was on board and securing the belt that would stop him falling out. The helicopter rose and was gone.

The four-man team were sat staring into space. They had failed just when the operation was going perfectly to plan; too good to be true? It certainly was; the only plus point was that the object had been destroyed or at least it appeared that way. It would be a few more hours before they made the carrier and then what? Would there services be no longer required?

The Pinger on Joe's arm made a sound; Joe read it and pulled a face. 'It looks like we are not going to make the carrier today. We are to divert to an alternate and get new orders there.'

'Roger that, we have the new route here,' the pilot said, indicating the display in front of him. The Blackhawk made a slow turn to the right and flew north-west towards the northern part of Ethiopia.

'Two hours,' the co-pilot said over the intercom, tapping the map on his knee. The passengers slept.

20.

The watchers noted that the individuals failed to determine the best way to retrieve it and that they were unable to counter the changes in mass that had been instigated, confirming that they had overestimated the level of intelligence at play. Their weapon had not destroyed the device; it had been removed as the high-intensity field had approached. It would be replaced at some time in the future. The watchers did not concern themselves anymore with this group; the effort they had seen expended did not alter what was to happen.

'Where are we going, Joe? Is it anywhere nice?' Tom had woken up to find that Joe was staring at him, perhaps willing him to waken.

'We are going to Aksum in the north of the country not that far from the boarder.'

'Isn't that supposed to be where the Ark of the Covenant is?'

'Indeed it is but I'm not sure that has anything to do with us or what we are expected to do as the building that is supposed to hold the Ark is on the other side of town from where we are going.'

The other two were now awake, roused by the conversation between Joe and Tom.

'Good time to set out what we are going to do for the next day or so. Can everyone hear me?'

There were three thumbs-up and Joe now had their attention; he explained that the orders so far were pretty vague but they were to land on the outskirts of Aksum over to the east of the town and await further orders. The chopper would not be staying with them so it was probably going to be time for a little stroll.

'Let's get fed and watered while we can. All take a dump and have a piss when we land; I'm assured that the drop-off point is secure and there is little danger of us being seen.' The four men rummaged around in the large ration container that was attached to the rear bulkhead. Each ate his fill and washed it down with water that was a little warm but good all the same.

The team began checking and double-checking their equipment; if they were to be landed and left they had better make sure that they had all they needed for at least a couple of days. Joe was receiving instructions again on the Pinger.

'Orders when we are on the ground.' Joe checked everyone had heard him then sat back with his eyes closed, deep in thought.

'Ten minutes!' The pilot indicated they were about to arrive. The tone of the rotor changed as they descended to fifty feet; the forward speed slowed and the aircraft seemed to make less noise than before. They could only see bush and a few larger trees out of the side-door window but they all knew that there would be numerous buildings of the sort that they had encountered in Asosa.

'Thirty seconds!' The pilot slowed the helicopter and Joe opened the side door; they were about ten feet from the ground. The Blackhawk touched down and the four men were out and running towards a row of small trees at the edge of a dried up water course that was filled with rubbish of all sorts. The Blackhawk was gone before they made the trees.

Joe briefed the team.

'OK, listen. We are on the outskirts of Aksum and we are to move around the edge of town in a westerly direction; the place we are looking for is the small church that is supposed to contain the Ark. Yes, I know, weird, isn't it? Once there we wait for darkness and then wait for midnight to arrive; after that we have to try and get a look at the Ark and report back. While we are waiting outside the church we monitor what the magnetic field is doing and report back. Well at least we have three machines as Tom's is a little bit broke.'

'How are we going to remain invisible to the locals? We are now out here bare-arsed in broad daylight and we have to wander about the town looking for the local church.' Tom was a little amazed that they hadn't been contacted already: big helicopter making loads of noise and four odd blokes having a chat at the local dump wasn't really normal.

'Yes, I know it was the first thing that came into my mind as I read the orders. Be assured, as I was, that we are not in any danger here and there will be no local interference; I would go as far to say that there are no locals in this area at all. It seems that they have been leaving over the last couple of weeks and now there is no one left.'

'That is around sixty thousand people; a major undertaking to get that many people to go, especially if some didn't want to leave. A logistical nightmare never mind the suffering that it would have caused.' Oliver was thinking about the major problems someone would have to even plan it.

'It seems, and I can only say what has been said to me, that something major happened here twenty days ago and no one wanted to stay; everyone has upped sticks and fled.'

Joe recounted what he had been learning from the data transmissions that he had been getting whilst on the helicopter. Stories of animals suddenly disappearing and people hearing strange noises in the night, even a group of armed men vanishing into thin air when they went outside to find out where the noise was coming from. Billy was thinking that here they were, a small group of armed men trying to discover what was going on. *Interesting…*

'So, is everyone ready? We should make a start and get to the other side of town before it gets dark.' They could easily manage that, of course; it would be ten hours before sundown and they had about five or six miles to go. Joe picked up his kit and made sure it was all secured on the harness he wore. The rest did the same and were soon ready for the off.

Oliver led this time with the three other men spaced out in the routine way, although it was thought that there would be no contact it was wise to do the dance as normal.

21.

Out in the Red Sea the *Ronald Reagan* was underway, performing a patrol route in a one-hundred-mile box. The guard force that supported it was at full readiness, ever watchful for anything that might pose a threat. The crews had been at this for days now and it looked like it would go on for some time. They had been ordered to maintain this alert until relieved by another carrier group in a few days, they would then head south and out into the Indian Ocean for some rest.

Down in the conference room, the professor and the colonel were sat with five other people discussing what had been going on, not only with the team that Joe was leading but three other teams that had been deployed in the area.

'Team three down in the south; what have we gained from them up to now?' The professor was asking the question but he was going to give the answer. Always full of rhetorical questions, as the colonel had quickly leaned. *It seems to be a way to gather his thoughts,* the colonel mused.

'Although the magnetic field jumped around all over the place when team three entered the closed area it didn't do anything to affect the four men; when they came back they had absolutely nothing to report. They did have some effect on the field but what it was telling us is unknown.'

The colonel glanced down at a small notebook that he had

been skimming through. 'Team one in the meantime has not reported back and did not make the pickup point. We must assume that we have lost them; there is no trace of them and even the tracker that the team leader's Pinger had on it is not communicating.'

'Was there any unusual activity before we lost contact?' The professor knew the answer but was asking for the benefit of the others gathered around the table.

'No, professor, nothing at all; they sent routine stuff to say they had arrived and were moving off, then nothing.' The colonel was a little dismayed at what he was saying; he had lost people before but he had always been on top of what they had been doing. He didn't like this one bit.

'Lastly we have team two with Joe and company, easily the most experienced team we have deployed.' The professor went over everything that Joe and his men had done and what they had reported back.

'They managed to pick up the object without a problem – very easily we thought at the time – but when they got it in to the helicopter, things started to go belly up. It appears that the object's mass increased and decreased under control of, as yet, an unknown mechanism, eventually having a mass so great that the Blackhawk was unable to maintain its position in the air. Once on the ground, however, the team were able to remove it and destroy it on the ground. Remember, this was the second time they had attempted to remove it from the cargo bay; why they succeeded the second time and not the first is a mystery.'

'Was the object destroyed, professor?' A big stocky man was speaking across the table.

'We do not know but the object was either destroyed or it went somewhere else. This was almost a rerun of previous incidents except this time Joe was standing a short distance away and wasn't harmed in any way, except having poor eyesight for a minute or so.' The professor brought up another image of magnetic fields onto the screen.

'Take a look at this and compare the timeline with what has been going on.' The magnetic field was shown to be very active around the time when team three was in the area and, although they didn't report any problems, something was happening. The chart showed a massive change at the time in discussion, only returning to normal when the team left the area.

'Now look at this one.' The magnetic changes in the area of team one were very, very extensive and peaked at about the time contact was lost, then suddenly back to normal levels of change.

'Lastly team two and the most interesting one.'

The chart showed a fairly flat field until the time that Joe and his team stepped from the helicopter when they first arrived where it then began building as they approached the town. It did a very large jump when the object was retrieved and remained in a fluctuating state until the moment the helicopter took off.

'This point is where Joe said they had put their magnetic fields generators in series over the object – you see that the overlying picture is one of calm. Then there is this.' The professor indicated a massive jump in the field strength. 'This is where the object got a little heavy for the Blackhawk and possibly dragged it to the ground. The team was then able to remove it and destroy it before getting away.'

Another chart overlaid onto a map came on the screen. 'This is the area around Aksum in the north of the country; you will see that the field strength is fairly low and consistent with what it should be with this level of sun activity.' The image changed and moved through a sequence showing the overall magnetic field with the town of Aksum in the middle. All around the field came and went and sometimes showed massive changes but over Aksum it didn't budge at all. It appeared that waves of field changes were sweeping past Aksum as if it was sheltered by something.

'The population of Aksum have now all left; they started to go a couple of weeks ago and nothing the local government could do would convince them to stay. As far as we know the only people in the area of Aksum today are our team two and the monks that guard and look after the church where the Ark of the Covenant is supposed to be. A little odd, don't you think?'

'It is more than odd, professor.' The colonel was on his feet looking closely at the screen. 'This looks like something you would see if you were assessing turbulence over a wing or around a tower when conducting vortex testing. So we have an area of calm in the middle of a much larger magnetic storm, for the want of a better word. What is doing this?'

'We all now agree that the cylindrical objects that have been arriving and the ones that have arrived in the past are something to do with it. We don't think that it is caused by the cylinders but that they have an element of control over how the field changes and adapts. The major question here is are we making things worse or better by removing them?' the professor said.

'At first, it was thought that the magnetic field was changing due to the actions of the objects and that the end result of this action could be the reduction or even the elimination of the Earth's magnetic field. It has been supposed that Mars suffered a similar fate sometime in the distant past and didn't manage to hold on to most of its atmosphere and died a very prolonged death through millions of years. Recent research, and we now have an almost limitless budget for this undertaking, has pointed in the direction of another explanation.' The thick set man was now in control of the imagery on screen and put up an image of Mars and the field overlaid.

'If we look at Mars' current magnetic field we can see that although the field is weak relative to Earth it has the same characteristics; a north and south pole with the field moving around the two. It also is affected by the Sun's activity, such as when there are solar flares. It behaves in the same way as Earth but on a much weaker level.' The slide changed to a more detailed one that was imaged over the planet's equator.

'See this little blip here, one of about twenty we have discovered. It is directly over the object that was found by the Sojourner Rover. We haven't the ability to investigate each blip but we expect that we did we would find one of these objects at each site.

'The field on Earth is showing similar blips that do relate to the object's position but what we don't have on Mars that we have here on Earth is the change in the field that we see at Aksum; for now this is the only place we have seen it.

'The conclusion we have reached is that the objects are not reducing the magnetic field in any way but rather they may even be bolstering the field for reasons unknown.' The image changed to yet another graph.

'Here we have the field strengths on a timeline when we removed the objects; you can see that every time the object was dealt with the field strength took a nose dive and was only restored when an increased output was detected from other objects around the globe.'

'What are the committee's recommendations then?' the professor asked. 'Are we to stop what we are doing and take a step back to see what happens? A risky scenario if the objects pose a real threat. Or do we carry on removing them and risk making matters worse?'

A man who previously had not spoken held his hand in the air to gain attention. 'At this point in time we do nothing new; team two are in Aksum and will continue with the investigation there. All other teams, less the team that is missing, have been withdrawn. We are to wait and see what team two comes up with and monitor the other areas to determine any changes for the good or otherwise.'

The group sat without saying anything; the colonel broke the silence. 'Gentlemen, at this point since we cannot move forward until we have more information, I suggest we break for some food. Are we all in agreement?' For once they were.

22.

Joe was looking at his watch. 'That's funny, my watch has stopped. Must have happened when I fired the weapon. Never mind, exact timing is unimportant at the moment.'

The four men had made good progress and were about ten minutes, at the current pace, from the area where the church was; so far they had encountered no one and no livestock, not even any dogs. The whole place was a bit unreal; it would normally be crowded with people going about their daily routine.

Billy was thinking. They had been into a few dwellings on the way but had not seen any sign of life; it was like the town had been constructed for a scene in a post-apocalyptic movie, except this town was real and had contained sixty thousand people a couple of weeks before. There had been a town here for thousands of years, what could make them all leave in so short a time?

Joe held up his hand and made the signal to stop; he wasn't sure why he was being so careful not to make a noise but old habits die hard and he couldn't help himself.

'We are now very close to where we need to be. All remember what the building looks like?' He looked around to confirm that they were all on the same song sheet.

'One thing is concerning me a little,' Tom said with a frown.

'Go on then, what is it, Tom?' Joe had been expecting this.

'The place where the Ark is supposed to be has been known about for some time; the building is not as old as the Ark of course but the mystery and legend surrounding this place is massive. For instance, since the Ark is so revered and financially very attractive, why has it not been taken or destroyed by the dozens of different bandit groups that have been in this area over the millennia?'

'Don't quite get that myself; it has always puzzled me that here we have the most famous and valuable item on the planet – at least to a large part of the population – and it just sits here guarded by a group of old monks who could not possibly defend it if someone tried to take it. But yet it is still here.'

'Perhaps it isn't.' Billy was stating the obvious, of course.

Joe thought that that might be the case but it wouldn't explain the difference in the field that surrounds it and the reason for the population to up sticks and leave. If the Ark isn't there then something else certainly was.

They all discussed this for some time, each offering theories from the lack of population to the Ark and what could be there if the Ark wasn't. The main agreement was if the Ark was causing the magnetic changes then they were about to stumble into something truly momentous. But if the Ark wasn't, and had never been there, what was? They were all about to take a very big step, for good or for worse, into the unknown.

The four team members collected their kit and made ready to continue. This time Oliver was to lead and Billy was bringing up the rear. The moved off in the direction of the church that was the target; they should be at the walls in around fifteen minutes. All four were taking their time as if none of them actually wanted to get to it. It was thought that the Ark was originally housed in the Church of Our Lady

Mary of Zion but had been moved during the time of the Emperor Haile Selassie to the purpose-built Chapel of The Tablet – at least that is what the story related. Another theory was that the chapel was a distraction and the Ark was still in or under the church. The team would soon find out.

The church was not as imposing as Joe thought it would be but it had a certain character to it. Certainly, it had seen better times with the roof in need of repair; there was a large amount of rubbish scattered at the sides and rear of the building. The front entrance was clear and tidy.

'It looks like we go into the front door then, gentlemen.' Oliver was still leading as they crossed the threshold and entered the church. It was very dark with little ambient light.

'Anyone got a magnetic warning?' Joe asked prompting the other three to suddenly become interested in the device they had.

'No, nothing,' they all said back.

'Spread out and have a look in every nook and cranny you can find. Remember, this is a church and a very important church for a lot of people; try not to break anything. If you find anything of interest give a shout. It seems that the monks who guard this place are absent. We can go and have a look in the chapel if this doesn't pan out.'

It took over an hour to make a meticulous search of the church. It was a very simple layout but had quite a few recesses in the walls and floors that had to be looked at. There was lots of religious iconography but nothing that could resemble the Ark. Plus there was no one in the building except them.

I wonder what the Ark really looks like; every time I picture it I see the Hollywood version. Maybe it is something altogether different and the accepted description is a ruse to misdirect. Joe was already thinking that there would not be anything of interest here in this building.

Billy was the last to return to the group by the door. 'Nothing at all, not even routine religious stuff you would find in any church that is in use on a daily basis. There is no paperwork, books, clothing or anything else that you would expect.'

'Onwards and upwards.' Joe led them out of the door they had come in; the brightness outside was stark compared to the darkness they become used to in the church.

'We will wait a couple of minutes to gather our thoughts and then will go and have a look at that.' Joe pointed across some open ground to a small square building. The building was the Chapel of the Tablet that the Emperor had built in the late fifties. 'Perhaps we will find something in there.' Joe was up and ready to go.

The four walked slowly across the area that separated the two buildings; the ground was mainly scrub with a few scraggy bushes growing in the dirt. There was no well-worn path you would expect to find in an area like this; it was if no one had ever walked this way. The building was not at all imposing, perhaps another indication that it did not contain anything, or was it to disguise the function of the chapel?

'Let's do a three-sixty on this then we will decide how we are to get in; the front door is not always the best entry point.' The four men spread out and went around the building checking all the external openings. The windows were quite high off the ground but could be managed with a leg up; they would have to do some damage, however, as the windows did not appear to be the kind that would open and certainly not from the outside.

They met at the front door. 'This is the only way in without doing some damage and damage we need to avoid, if possible.' Joe had made his mind up; they would knock on the front door and go in.

'Ready everyone?' Joe gave the door three strong raps. They all listened; nothing happened, only silence from the inside. Joe tried again; nothing.

'In we go then,' Joe said as he pushed on the door; it opened very easily despite its size, the hinges being well balanced and oiled. It required little effort to push the door wide. All four peered into the gloom that was all they could determine of the inside of the chapel.

'Head torches, I think.' Billy switched his lamp on and the rest followed suit.

The beams from the torches didn't penetrate the gloom for more than a couple of metres but it was certainly better than nothing.

'I think we should stay within sight for this one; there are supposed to be people in here that have sworn an oath to protect the Ark no matter what. Let us hope that that part of the story is just that, a story.

A voice came from the darkness; calm but questioning. 'What language is that?' Billy was asking Oliver who wasn't exactly sure.

'Sounds a bit like Amharic but it's not; I know it's an old language from this area called Ge'ez, a precursor of the modern Amharic that is spoken widely in Ethiopia. It is still used by some of the Christians hereabouts.'

'But what is he saying?' Joe was still not able to see who was speaking but it certainly sounded like a man. By tradition only males were allowed in this area anyway.

'I have no idea; for all but two words it was unintelligible.'

The voice boomed again. 'Why are you here?' English this time, a non-regional accent.

'Didn't learn the language in the States or anywhere there is a strong inflection on the English. Quite odd.' Oliver was very interested now.

'Can we see you and speak face-to-face? We mean you no harm.' Joe thought he sounded a little trite but he meant what he said, he didn't mean any harm.

A man stepped into the light; he seemed to suddenly appear and looked like he was a hundred years old.

'Why are you here?' The man said again but this time the voice sounded American. *Somewhere from the mid-west at a guess,* Oliver thought.

'Why are you here?' This time the accent was from the north-east of England.

'We are looking for something, sir, perhaps you can help us.' Joe thought he should at least answer the question.

'I cannot be of help to you and your team; you should go.' The voice was still calm but the accent mimicked Joe's.

'Why do you change accents when you speak?' Oliver butted in.

'I can speak all languages of the Earth and can converse with all mankind in their own tongue.'

Impressive to say the least if it was true. Oliver was beginning to think it might be a bit verbal sleight of hand.

'I feel that you doubt me.' He was looking directly at Oliver.

'No, not at all but I have never heard of anyone who has the language skills that you have.'

'It is better that I am able to communicate with any man that might come here, if I can speak the way they do it is better. Language here on Earth is rudimentary and not difficult to learn. I ask you again; why are you here?'

Joe stepped forward, not fully knowing what he was to say. 'We are searching for information; we are scientists and are trying to discover why the magnetic field in this area is different from what we would expect.'

Joe thought that this might be a bit random for the old

man to grasp but he had to say something and this was the truth.

'What you seek here has always been here, even before the time of man.'

'That leaves out the Ark then; man have been here in Africa for a considerable time longer than the Ark.' Billy was thinking out loud. 'That is if the Ark actually exists.'

'The Ark you speak of does exist but you cannot see it.' The old man was still very calm and unmoving; he held Joe's gaze, unblinking.

'Excuse us while we go outside and speak about this.' Joe moved away towards the door; the other three followed Joe outside.

'Not sure what we are to do about this. We have clear instructions about getting here and investigating but they are a little vague when it comes to dealing with the locals and in particular the guardian of the Ark, if that is what this old chap is.'

Joe was inputting something into the Pinger; perhaps a more detailed instruction would be given now they were here.

'The old man is not a threat as far as we can tell; he must weigh all of fifty kilograms wet through. Shall we simply ignore him and do the search?' Oliver was outlining a plan that might work but what if the old man was just the front of a considerable defence set up?

'Was there any magnetic activity that showed on the sensors.' Joe thought he should have asked that when they were inside.

'No, nothing at all; I was monitoring my device the whole time – not a beep,' Oliver said, getting a nod from the other two.

The Pinger gave a sound; the answer had come. Joe read the instructions and looked up.

'We are to search the building and ignore any occupants that try and prevent us; we are authorised to use minimum force if necessary.' None of them thought it a good idea to start wrestling with an old man but it may be needed.

'Just a thought, but when we go back in can I do the talking? I have an idea about this chap which may solve our problems.' Oliver had obviously seen something the rest had not.

'Oliver to lead, we will follow and say nothing. Let Oliver speak for us.'

Oliver went towards the door, which was now closed again; Oliver thought that it was left open but wasn't sure. He pushed the door and again it opened without effort; very quiet. They were all stood in the entrance way where they had been before.

The man appeared as before and spoke in Ge'ez just as before. Oliver held his arm up to make sure no one said anything. The old man continued in the same language.

'*Qui êtes-vous?*' Oliver spoke in French.

'I am the custodian. What do you want?' the old man replied in French.

Oliver said nothing but walked directly at the man and walked right through him.

'Not real, a projection or hologram of some sort, this is really interesting.' Oliver said smiling.

'What do you want?' The old man had returned to English.

'You see, he is responding to what we do and say; when we came back through the door he started at the beginning and switched from language to language depending on what we said. This is very clever and does not belong here in the middle of nowhere.'

'Not that clever, he is an automated meet-and-greet person; he would be on minimum wages if the was real.' Billy was throwing in his opinion.

'If he was here historically it would certainly have frightened off the casual visitor but that in itself raises some interesting questions. This is not ancient technology; at least not from our perspective.' Billy was right of course this was unlikely to be old, unless there was much more to the story. They may be in some danger.

'What do you want?' The old man was still talking and looking at them.

'Tom, shut the door and see what happens to the old-timer,' Joe said.

Tom walked back a few paces and closed the door.

'What do you wa—' The old man was gone.

'Triggered by the door opening but it must have been listening to know what language was in use and it did interact with Joe when he was talking.' Oliver was scouting the immediate area to see if the projection source was there. He couldn't find it.

Joe raised his hand for silence. 'Since we are still here in the building and the first obstacle has gone we should search this place from top to bottom; it is not as big as the church so shouldn't take that long. Remember, give a shout if you find anything, and I mean anything.'

They split up and went further into the chapel, the lights from their head torches illuminating the walls as they progressed. The chapel was a hollow square with nothing in it. At least it appeared to be that way. The windows were covered in a fairly thick cloth that didn't let in any light.

'What do you want?' Tom was at the rear wall of the chapel when the old man reappeared; he looked exactly the same but this time spoke in English from the off.

'The old guy has come back, Joe,' Tom said and began to go around the image to carry on the search.

The old man moved so quickly that Tom was taken

completely by surprise; in no time at all Tom was overbalanced and found himself heading for the floor. The old man stood over him. 'What do you want?'

Tom picked himself up, a little embarrassed that such an old man could easily throw him; he hadn't been overmatched in that way since he first took up judo when he was ten. Tom noticed that there was a door directly behind the old man; it was on the outer wall and he couldn't remember a door in that position when the scouted the outside.

All four were now in front of the old man who didn't seem to be at all perturbed about the odds that were now facing him.

'What do you want?' It was the same flat voice as before.

'Do you remember when we first encountered this chap he asked, "Why are you here?" but then he went onto, "What do you want?" Perhaps he is modifying the question to get the answer; a little bit like a teacher would when asking a question the student doesn't understand; a bit like, "Can you rephrase the question, please?" except he is doing it without being asked.' *Oliver has his teaching head on*, Billy thought to himself.

'He does have a physical presence now, which I tell you is very real; he threw me without any effort, like a textbook throw against a complete novice, except I am certainly no novice. If he was an Olympic athlete he would certainly be in the medals.'

'We will try talking again; it worked for a short time at the door.' Joe moved to speak to the old man.

'Excuse us but we are looking for information regarding a magnetic field that has been detected inside this building; we must find out what it is doing and make a report.' The old man looked at Joe then moved his gaze to each in turn.

'You are not the people who are here often but are an unknown; I will have to confer with my master. Wait here; do not proceed further, wait for my return.' The old man moved slightly to his right and was gone. Maybe it was still a projection.

'Not much of a conversationalist is he, and how did he go so quickly?' Oliver was looking at the door that had been behind the old man; it had one large lever on the left-hand edge but no other furniture or markings. It was made from wood that looked like it had been recycled from some earlier construction but very solid all the same, even the hinges were hidden.

Suddenly the door opened making Oliver jump back in surprise; in the doorway stood a figure, the same old man as before. Was it another projection?

'Who leads you?' The voice was soft and non-aggressive.

'I do, my name is Joe.'

The man looked at Joe as if he was thinking of something to say; he then looked each in turn before ending with Billy.

'You will come with me,' he said and turned to leave through the door.

'Go for it, Billy, we don't want to argue the pecking order at this stage. Be very careful, I would suggest the Glock first then the EDW if it goes tits up.'

Billy followed the old man into the doorway and on into whatever was behind. The door closed and there was complete silence. Oliver thought he could hear his own heart beating; he didn't like it when his brother was out of touch.

'That door, I would suggest cannot go anywhere, we all went around the outside of this building and this is the rear outside wall.' Joe pointed to the wall with the door in it. 'There cannot be a room or space that would hold two people. The walls are not thick enough to hold a space the size of what we saw beyond that door; this is odd, very odd. If the door led to the outside we would have seen daylight but we did not. This gets better all the time. Let's have a good look at the door and see how it might open.'

Joe put his shoulder to the wood and pushed; nothing moved. The handle on the left side was decorative and didn't move; he would have had similar reaction if he had pushed against the wall. There had been no sound when the door had closed, no moving of a locking mechanism or even the sound of the door meeting the frame.

'All we can do now is wait and hope for good outcome. I suggest that we have another look around this place to see what we can find.' The three moved off and looked around the other parts of the chapel.

Billy was walking behind the old man; they were in a corridor that was very narrow and they would not be able to pass should anyone come the other way. Billy wasn't expecting anyone else, however. As the door had closed behind them the warning lights on Billy's arm began to blink. The indication of a magnetic field was clear but the third light was also on. What were they told about the third light? 'If this one comes on you are to evacuate immediately.' *Fantastic I will do that, of course.* The corridor echoed with the sound of his footsteps, the old man didn't make any noise; he gave the impression that he was gliding just above the surface of the floor. Billy released the strap over his pistol. *Better safe than sorry*, he thought to himself.

After a short while the old man stopped at another door; it was the same design and construction as the one in the back wall of the chapel. The old man didn't stop but went straight through the door opening as he got close. Once they were through, the door closed behind them as silently as the first.

Billy thought that his eyes were getting used to the gloom but soon realised that the light level within this space was increasing. The level continued to rise until it began to be uncomfortably bright; Billy had to screw up his eyes to be able to see. It was now painfully bright.

They were in a room that was twenty feet square at most; the walls were bare and there were no windows or doors other than the one behind them that they had entered through. The ceiling was maybe only ten feet above them; it was as bare as the walls without any discernible colour or pattern; the atmosphere had a dusty, old smell. In the middle of the room was a raised platform about a foot high and was as square as the floor plan. Billy thought that the temperature in the room was around twenty-one degrees celcius; quite comfortable. The air was very dry.

The old man was looking at him. 'Behold! This is what you and many others have been seeking.'

Billy looked around the room and walked along the side of the raised platform. 'I don't see anything.'

'As you will know the Ark, as you refer to it, is held in this place and had been in the grounds of the church for some time. Legend has it that a monk from the church is dedicated to watching over it until he dies; then he will be replaced by another and so on. Only the monk who guards is ever allowed to see it and once he has seen it he must never leave the sanctuary of the chapel.'

'What happens if the man who guards does leave?' Billy thought the conversation was a little odd as there was obviously nothing here to guard.

'He who guards cannot leave until he is called to a better life; he will then be replaced by another.'

'What would happen if I forced you to leave?' Billy didn't think there would be any circumstance where he thought to do that of course but he asked anyway.

'It is not possible for you or anyone else to remove me until I am called; then I will be replaced.'

OK, Billy thought, *I will ask the obvious question*. 'Where is the Ark as it is not here? This is an empty room.'

'The room is not empty; you and I are here, as is the Ark. I see this puzzles you; your own legends say that only I am allowed to view the Ark and that it must be hidden from all others.'

'Yes but you have not answered my question. Where is the Ark?'

The old man smiled. 'It is here in front of you but you are not allowed to see it. The Ark is always here, it does not move anywhere else. I am here to watch over it, I can see it, and you cannot.'

Billy was getting a little distracted with this conversation and had forgotten that they were not looking for the Ark specifically but were investigating the strange magnetic field that was present in this place. He looked at the warning lights on his arm; the power light was still on but the other two were not illuminated; he half covered them with his hand to see if the light in the room was obscuring them. They were definitely off so no magnetic field and no shifting around.

Billy changed tack. 'Why did you choose me over the other three to come in here?'

'Your intellect made you the most suitable to be able to grasp what I have shown you.'

Billy got it alright. There were two possibilities: one, the Ark was not here and never was, or, two, the Ark is here but it projected that much power and control that only this old man was allowed to view it. Was it real or was it a trick? Billy wouldn't bet money on either.

'Is there anything else in this building?' Billy thought that it was likely that there was because if the background magnetic field, or the lack of it, that showed on the global scans.

'There is nothing in this room except the Ark, you and me,' said the old man. Billy noted that he had put the Ark at the front of the pecking order but had left himself to last.

'Why is the Ark here and not somewhere else?'

'This place was chosen to receive the Ark many, many years ago; it is a special place because the Ark can be hidden here away from its enemies. It will not move from here.'

'Well hopefully I will live to a ripe old age then.' Billy thought that he had found out all he could and it was time to go. 'One last thing; what do you know of the people who have left the town? Why have they suddenly left?'

'You already know that answer.' The old man said matter-of-factly. 'The large changes in the magnetic field you have been investigating, along with the cylinders that have been falling to Earth.'

'You know about the cylinders?'

'The cylinders have been falling to Earth for longer than the Ark has been here, but yes I do know of the cylinders; they are part of the reason the people of the town have gone.'

'Why so?' Billy was getting somewhere, at least he thought so.

'The nature of the cylinders has changed; they now start to control things that are not controlled; things like the weather and the land and sea. They are a danger to all.'

'But what is to be done about them?' Billy didn't suppose for one minute the old man would tell him exactly how the threat could be avoided but you never know.

'You must go, the answer to what you seek is not here. I am but one in a long line of guardians that have seen many things; the Ark will endure despite anything that will happen from now.'

The door behind them was open and the old man led Billy into the tight corridor; the lights on his arm were on again. The door that led into the chapel was opening as they approached. The old man stopped just inside the entrance and indicated that Billy should go through.

'Take care, friend, you are all in danger.' The door closed and the old man was gone. The other three crowded round, all eager to know what Billy had been doing; he had been gone for more than two hours.

'It seems that the Ark is in the room at the end of this cor...' Billy indicated with his hand but stopped mid word. The door was not there, only an uninterrupted wall that went both ways from where they were. They all shone their torches around; the door had gone.

'Oh dear. As I was saying the Ark is in there, wherever there is, but it cannot be seen by anyone except the old man.'

'So you didn't see it then?' Joe was curious that Billy had just accepted that he was not allowed to look at it.

'Actually I'm not sure it is in there as it was just an empty room with a raised platform in the middle of it on which, presumably, the Ark stands. The meaning being is that because I am not allowed to see it I cannot see it, although it is there. It may be a case of the emperor's new clothes or it maybe not visible to the likes of me.

'The old man did say things about the cylinders, however. He said that they had been arriving for millennia and that they were a danger to all. It seems that they are interfering with the elements in some way. He wasn't a fan of them; he said they were the reason why the whole town has done a runner. He also said that I was picked because I was the brightest.' Billy smiled.

'Had the old man been drinking, Billy?' Oliver also smiled.

'This place isn't special because the Ark is here but the Ark was brought here because the place is special. The old man said that it was the only place where the Ark would be safe and protected from its enemies. The building, of course, is relatively new, built over a site that has always had a special meaning.'

'Let us get this straight; the cylinders are a danger, not only to the planet in general but also to the Ark and the people who look after it. Where the Ark is concerned they have, in this place, something that has protected and is protecting it and them. Roger so far?' Joe was outlining what they may have learned from Billy's trip into the room at the rear of the chapel.

'If we are here then we are safe from whatever the cylinders are doing?' Oliver was not convinced they were not on a wild goose chase but he was open to argument.

'Well if we go by the changes in magnetic field here and outside we seem to be in dead zone as far as sudden magnetic changes are concerned.'

Joe was inputting information into the Pinger; if they couldn't make a decision than he was sure the control would. 'That's that then, I suggest we have a look around in the closest houses and see if we can get some food.' As they walked away from the chapel the warning lights on the devices blinked on and off.

'Random fluctuations again.' Oliver was taking particular interest in his device. 'Nothing to worry about; no high levels but jumping about all the same.'

23.

'What do you mean he's gone?' The security chief was talking on the phone to the team leader that had charge of David Smith. Mr Smith had been there for a couple of weeks and was a person of exceptional interest; he was not without an observer at any time but it seems that he had managed to escape. The chief knew that this was not going to end well; he had never "lost" a subject before.

'Big Dave had been in the interrogation loop the whole time he had been here and it had gone very well; he was not obstructive or in any way defensive. Quite the contrary, he had been most helpful as if he was trying to determine the truth as much as the team was. But now he was gone.'

'Have you instigated the protocols?' The chief was trying to control his voice and not shout down the phone; he was failing and was started to think about panic. This Mr Smith had been given number one priority; not just in the interrogation but in everything he did; it was all to be monitored and recorded.

'Yes, sir, we have; he shouldn't be able to get far before we pick him up.'

'Shouldn't be able to get far? You idiot, he shouldn't be gone at all – find him and quickly.'

David Smith was not far away; he was stood at the side of the river that ran past the facility; a facility that had held him prisoner since he was picked up in the Welsh valley. He still didn't fully understand what was going on but as the days went by he knew more and more. Now it was time for him to leave. What was driving him to leave he did not know but it had become irresistible and now he was here; he had learned all he could from the people at the facility. The sun was shining and he felt very well with not a care in the world.

'How did he get out?' The chief was in the control room where the team were reviewing the data recordings from just before it was noticed that Big Dave was gone. The screen showed David lying on his bed, seemingly asleep; nothing was happening in the room.

'How long was he sleeping?'

'He turned in just after ten last night; this point is just after six this morning.' The whole team was looking at the image and watching the time shown at the bottom of the screen; it was passing at three times normal. Big Dave was obviously a deep sleeper as he didn't move at all. This had been noted early on, he went to sleep and didn't move at all until he got out of bed in the morning; unusual but not unknown behaviour.

The clock was just passing ten minutes past seven when Dave was suddenly out of bed and standing looking at the camera. 'Wind that back and run it in real time,' the chief said. Big Dave was back in bed; his eyes opened and he rolled over and sat up; he then got out of bed and walked over to stand under the camera, looking directly at it.

'He hasn't done that before; the cameras are all hidden, it would take an expert a long time to find them; the object lens is tiny and hidden in the paint work.'

'He has his clothes on! When did he do that?' The technician was speaking and without prompting rewound the image and ran it in slow time. Dave got out of bed wearing only shorts and a tee shirt but as he walked across the room he was suddenly dressed in combat fatigues; paused to look at the camera then seemed to evaporate and was gone. The technician ran it back and forth but only confirmed that the clothing on Big Dave suddenly changed from one to the other, and then he was no longer in view.

'Weirdest thing I have ever seen. I have to inform the control; get that segment ready for transmission.' The chief left the room even more concerned than he was before.

In the southern end of the Red Sea the carrier group was on the northern leg of the circuit it was maintaining; the professor and the colonel were in the conference room discussing the progress or otherwise of the team in Aksum. They had decided to leave the team there for now and see what has been happening in other parts of the world. It did not look good; they seem to be having a run around but for what reason was unclear. Several teams had been withdrawn and some had been left in place; the team that had not reported was still missing.

There was a knock at the door and a marine major walked in without being asked. 'This just came for you, colonel.' The major turned and left.

The marine had left an envelope that contained a USB stick and one piece of paper; the colonel read the sheet and handed it to the professor. 'Looks like things are getting interesting, professor, your man David has done a runner.' The colonel liked the way that the Brits used these odd phrases and used them himself whenever he could.

The professor walked over the terminal on the disc and plugged in the stick; a code entry image came up; the professor entered the nine-digit code that he had memorised the day before. Codes changed every day and were sometimes very difficult to commit to memory but this one he had mastered in a few minutes, perhaps his brain was getting used to the sequencing.

A black and white image came onto the main screen; it was the footage taken at the facility in France and showed Big Dave in bed, seemingly asleep. He then woke, turned in the bed and got up. He stood in the room for a couple of seconds then moved towards the camera and looked directly at it; then he was gone.

'How did he do that with the clothes?' Both men were puzzled by what they had seen. The professor was reading the paper again.

'We have seen what the investigation team saw; they offer no explanation except that what we saw actually took place; nothing has been edited from this sequence. He got out of bed, got dressed in less than a tenth of a second and left the room but did not use the door and now he is missing; they have searched the facility and the surrounding area. He is not there and he could not have gotten out of the exclusion area in the time he had. But then again he couldn't have gotten out of the room, but he did.'

'What did we learn from him before he ran?' The colonel was calling up the file on Big Dave. 'Not a great deal except that he was not obstructive and his interrogators thought that he was cooperating fully when he was answering the questions. But aside from the differences in DNA that we have already talked about he does seem to have a complete overhaul. Previously he had a touch of arthritis in his right shoulder, which stemmed from an earlier injury but the arthritis is gone and so is any sign of the injury.'

'Not sure what more we could have done with him; he was in one of the most secure facilities we have and he simply left. Do we know where he is now?'

The professor was reading the small print at the bottom of the page. 'We would if he hadn't left this behind.' He indicated the last line in the bottom paragraph.

It detailed the results of a search of his room when he absconded; a small electrical device was found in his bed; a chip that could be used to determine his location anywhere on the planet. It was of a new series of trackers that had been under development for some time and this one was not only implanted under the skin but was actually deep into his femur. He didn't even know it was there as it had been placed when he was sedated when he first arrived. He had however managed to remove it – not an easy task and quite impossible without losing some blood. There was no blood on the bed or in the room; there wasn't even any trace of him on the chip itself.

'Are we sure this is the same chip that was put inside him?' The colonel asked the question.

The professor checked the notes again. 'Yes or one that is identical to the one implanted, which is not possible as there are none that are close to each other for obvious reasons. We cannot have two or three getting confused by the tracking device. On the tracker, David Smith shows as being where the chip is.'

'So, he removed a chip that he couldn't, wore clothing that he did not have, and left a room that he couldn't leave. Interesting.' The colonel was reading the notes from top to bottom again.

Big Dave was still not far away but for some reason there didn't seem to be anyone looking for him; hiding in plain sight where the best concealment always was. He didn't know what was expected of him but he was very calm, in fact, he thought he was the calmest he had ever been – not a single care in the world.

The watchers were changing the plan; they had deployed the individual that they had returned; this was not intended at the beginning but the others had discovered the relevance of the hidden place or it seemed that they had. The watchers had to act or the sequence would be compromised and they would be out of time. What should they do now?

'We will move the individual to each location in turn and it can correct the sequence.'

'It must be done or it will take many rotations to arrive back at the start.'

Big Dave was back in the Welsh valley; again he stood by the gaping hole that had been Site A. It was still the same, even the drone was still flying overhead. He looked at the drone and was transported to Site B in an instant.

The operator of the drone camera only caught a very brief image of David as he looked at the camera in the slightly unnerving way he had done so before; then he was gone. The operator ran the images back and forth; he was there one second and gone the next. The operator pressed the alarm button that was next to the control panel. It was too late David Smith was already at Site B.

The control room was working at full capacity; they had been analysing all the data that had been retrieved from most of the field units. The only exceptions were the team that had gone missing and the one led by Joe in Aksum. There was a live link to the conference room on the *Ronald Reagan*; the professor could see the group he was talking to quite clearly.

'Where is David now?' The professor was asking; at this point he had no reason to be alarmed, in fact, he was very curious as to how David had gotten from France to the Welsh countryside so quickly. But all of that could wait because it seemed that David had again disappeared, but where to?

There was a commotion at the side of the room that the professor couldn't see on the monitor. The technician that was sat at the terminal turned around to look; he obscured even more of the room. 'What is going on? Please pay attention or we will be here all, day.'

The technician didn't answer; he was looking open-mouthed at Big Dave as he came into the room by the side door, or rather David had appeared at the side door as if he had come through but that door was locked and didn't open for anyone. The sentry challenged David and walked towards him, a pistol aimed at David's chest.

'You must stop what you are doing.' David's voice was very calm, as if he was talking about the weather.

'Hold it right there, fella, and we can have a discussion about this.' The guard with the gun was still advancing on David who was head and shoulders taller than he was; didn't matter he had a firearm and would take this big guy down, no problem.

David turned and reached out to a woman standing against the room wall; he only touched her briefly on the elbow but her whole arm suddenly took on a dark smokey texture, it travelling up her arm and soon her whole body was engulfed; the last piece of her to go was her face, which showed no signs of stress or fear just puzzlement. The smokey image then dissolved and drifted away; the woman was gone.

The sentry fired two rounds into Big Dave's chest: it had no effect, the two projectiles doing no damage at all – that's if they ever reached their target.

Pandemonium erupted inside the room with everyone trying to get out of the way of either David or the man with the gun. The gun fired twice more but this time David was very close to the sentry: the two bullets had no effect. David reached out and touched the guard's gun; it and the guard went the same way as the woman: there was nothing left.

David Smith walked over to the terminal that had the live link to the professor who was yelling into the microphone trying to get a response from the technician. The technician was past answering questions; he was frightened witless by what he had seen at such close range. David paused to let the technician get out of the way; he then sat down and looked into the camera that was on top of the monitor.

'Professor, it's been a long time.' Then after a second's pause. 'You must stop what you and your teams are doing; you cannot alter what is to be.'

'If we cannot alter what is to be, whatever that is, then why should we stop? It will make no difference so why do you insist?'

There was the briefest of smiles that crossed David's face; he leant forward and touched the monitor with the end of a finger. The screen at the professor's end went blank then showed only static.

'What do we make of that?' The professor was very puzzled by what he had just seen.

The door opened and marine corporal came in. 'The coms link to Site B has dropped out, professor, and we cannot get it back; the primary link indicator is no longer there, never seen this sort of thing before.'

'Keep working on it, please, and let me know if you determine why it dropped, thank you.' That was the indicator for the corporal to leave.

'Let's get the drone over Site B and see what is going on.' The colonel was speaking into a handset that was linked to the control element for the drone deployment.

The professor was playing back what had just transpired; forwards and back and at one frame at a time they relived what had gone on.

'The way it happened to the guard looks similar to what happened to the objects when we viewed their disappearance in slow time; gets a little fuzzy then is gone.' The professor was rewinding and watching the sequence again.

'Yep, see that? David just touches the muzzle of the pistol

then the image changes resolution; this change then moves from the end of the barrel through the gun and into the guard's hand. It happened within two seconds at most.'

'Look at this, colonel; David doesn't touch the camera but somewhere further down on the monitor, my face at a guess.'

'It is getting serious now and we still don't know what we are dealing with; although David is indicating that we do because he wants us to stop.' The professor went on, 'What are we doing that is having an effect? Well we have destroyed or removed several cylinders from around different places; one removal resulted in a whole site going with it. Maybe it is the removal of the cylinders that they do not like and the fact we are not leaving them alone is the problem for them.'

'Are we dealing with a "them", professor?'

'We don't, of course, but it is the easiest label we can attach to what is going on.'

The phone rang once; the colonel picked it up and listened then put it down without saying anything. 'We have the feed from a drone over Site B, professor.' The colonel changed the source for the picture on the monitor and the area that Site B occupied came into view.

'Is this live, colonel?'

'Almost; about a two second delay as the signal is routed but close enough.'

The scene the drone was watching over did not look out of the ordinary. The buildings on Site B were all still there and the transport that ferried people around was still parked where you would expect it; the perimeter fence seemed to be intact.

'What do you see, professor?' Both men were watching the screen intently.

'I cannot see anything that is different from when I visited a month or so ago.'

'It's not what we can see but what we cannot, professor;

there are no people, none at all.' The colonel zoomed in the image to confirm what he was saying. 'Even the motor pool vehicle line is without personnel.'

The colonel picked up the phone that was connected directly to the operations room in New York. The other end answered. 'Colonel Johnson, United States Marine Corps, Alpha, Quebec, Delta, three, four, zero, four, seven, one, four, two; confirm.' The operator at the other end confirmed the colonel's access code.

'Site B has been compromised and is to be put under a code five restriction.' The colonel put the phone down and looked at the professor. 'All happening now, it seems; we will get an idea of what has been going on at Site B in an hour or so. Hopefully David is still there so we can close this thing down; if he has gone then who knows.'

The professor was speaking over the link to the control committee that was somewhere in the United States; he explained what had gone on and what his team had deduced from it. The overall plan was still to restrict access to the cylinders and try and retrieve one if possible. The professor didn't agree with this and thought it might be prudent to take a step back and wait, that way they may be better placed to see what is happening and get an idea of what part the cylinders, both modern and ancient, have to play. The committee did not agree and ordered that the teams that had been withdrawn were to proceed.

The watchers had removed the individual that had been held and had moved him to the place that was one of the control points. It had worked well; the place was no longer a threat but there were other places that had to be dealt with if the plan was to reach fruition in the allotted time. They would move him to the control place that was on the sea. Once that was removed the sequence could resume.

David found himself in the alleyway that led to the main conference room on the *Ronald Reagan*; he had never been on a ship this big before but he knew where he had to go. There were only two of them that he had to deal with; he could then move on.

David was not aware of Lily who had watched him appear and move down towards the conference room that held the colonel and the professor. David moved past the storeroom that most of the specialised kit was kept and stopped at the door for the conference room.

'Excuse me, sir, you are in a restricted area. Can I ask your business and see some authorisation?' A very large marine had intercepted David who gave the impression that he had not heard the challenge.

'Need some help here.' The marine was speaking into a microphone that was attached to his lapel.

David turned to face the guard, his hands by his side. 'You are not what I have come for; please do not stop me.' David held the marine's gaze.

As the marine came closer he drew his sidearm, a modified Glock, and took aim at David. 'Stop where you are, do not move.'

David moved very fast and reached out and touched the end of the pistol; the gun, the marine's arm and then the marine dissolved. In less than a second the marine had gone. David turned to face the door.

'Give me one of those!' Lily was in the store that David had just walked past. She was pointing to the EDW that was at the end of the nearest shelf. The tone in Lily's voice left no doubt in the storeman's mind that he should comply. He then went round the back and removed a battery and cable unit from the charging array.

'The pack is not fully charged; should be good for two discharges though.'

'Let's hope so, or this could end in tears.'

Lily turned and walked out of the room, David was still at the door, looking at it.

'David, stop!' Lily had powered up the EDW and was pointing it at David; she had used his first name although he wouldn't have known her but it might distract him a little more than just shouting. She wasn't sure what would happen if she discharged this thing in such a confined space but it would certainly stop David – at least she hoped it would. She had just finished watching the footage of David working at Site B.

David turned and started to raise his right hand but as he did so his whole shape blurred and evaporated; nothing of him was left.

Lily went to the door and entered the room; both the colonel and the professor were sitting at a desk in the corner. 'Were you aware of what just happened outside, professor? Colonel?' The two men had not; they had heard the guard's challenge but thought it was likely a crewman had entered the restricted area by mistake; it had happened only the day before when a new member of the engineering team had got lost.

Lily quickly filled them in on the detail of what had transpired just a few feet away from where they were.

'How the hell did he get here? Thousands of miles in minutes – is that even possible?'

'Lily, you say that you only pointed the weapon at him but did not fire it?'

'Yes, professor, I only told him to stop and aimed the EDW; he looked at me then disappeared.'

'What about the sentry outside?' The colonel knew he had lost another of the team.

'He just became fuzzy and then he was gone. There was no noise at all.' Lily powered down the weapon on her arm.

Despite an extensive search no sign of David was found; the guard had also left no trace outside the door where he had met his end. How David had arrived and left was a puzzle.

'I think we owe our lives to Lily.' The professor was getting tired and it showed in his face. 'If she hadn't deployed the EDW I think David would have been in here amongst us. It is odd that to merely indicate the weapon was to be fired was enough to put him off. It seems that we have a weapon that does intimidate them; I'm saying "them" again but who knows.'

The watchers were puzzled. 'They have become more aware than we expected.' One said to the other. 'They are deploying the weapon more often; it will soon pose a threat to the outcome that is planned.'

'The plan must proceed, there can be no other way; if it does not, the sequence will not complete and it must. We will move to the other places and remove the ones that can be removed; we will return here at the end.'

24.

Joe and his team were about half a mile from the chapel that held the Ark; at least it was supposed to hold the Ark but from what Billy had reported they all thought that if the Ark was there, then it wasn't on show.

Every dwelling they entered was the same; everything in place except the items that you expect to be taken if the occupants had left in a hurry but had the intention of returning in the not-too-distant future; they even found some refrigeration still running. The local grid was still supplying electricity in most of the houses.

'OK fellas, let's take what we need and leave the rest; no unnecessary damage. Don't take anything that we do not need immediately. We can call for extraction later on when the professor makes his mind up as to what he wants us to do.'

The four men had found enough for their needs; some dates and flat bread, even some dried fish that was really good. They all sat outside a house that was bigger than usual and appeared to be some sort of administration centre for this part of town. There was a large mosque across the road with the doors wide open giving a view of the inside; there were no other people present as far as they could tell.

The Pinger on Joe's arm beeped once. 'It looks like Big Dave is on the move; he has absconded from the place in France and has been on the carrier with the professor. It is not good news; several personnel presumed killed and David is to be treated as hostile; it looks like he is the enemy now. They are not sure but think that the EDW should be the weapon of choice.'

'What! I have known Big Dave for donkey's years and I cannot believe he would turn – not a chance.' Tom did not believe the narrative that Joe was giving.

Joe was still reading. 'Well he is on film removing several people and is suspected of doing the same to a guard on the *Ronald Reagan* so we will take all this info at face value and keep our eyes open. Be ready for Big Dave or anybody else turning up unannounced from now on.'

The four men chatted about what could be happening with David Smith. He had been appearing in odd places it seems; first in Wales then on the carrier, where he couldn't have, and now they are being warned about him out here in the middle of nowhere.

David Smith was watching them; they were unaware, of course, as he was nearly a mile away up on the small hill that sat at the western edge of town; his vision had even improved from when he was in the Welsh valley. He didn't know how but he wasn't tired and felt as fit as he ever had; even from when he was in training to join at Hereford and that was some years ago. He had to stop these four but was unsure how he would do it; three of them had a weapon that could stop him, the fourth was carrying a broken one. David wasn't sure why Joe was carrying the defective device but it would give him an advantage when they all came together.

'Let's get back to the church and chapel area; it will be easier to get the chopper in there than here amongst the houses.' They all made ready to move; they would leave everything as they had found it, less the food and water but they only took what they needed in the short term.

'Big Dave has appeared unannounced twice now so we should expect that he may turn up here even though he was a thousand miles away only a couple of hours ago; they don't know how he does it but he is doing it; eyes open, everyone. Let's set the standard walking routine from now on.' The four men spread out; all within sight of the other but not close enough for more than one to get a burst of incoming fire should it happen.

Billy saw him first; David was stood at the corner of the last house before the open ground that had the church and chapel in the middle of it. He was just standing, watching them come up the road. Joe signalled to stop. 'Tom, you know him better than the rest of us; go and see what he is about; we will cover you from here.'

Tom took his backpack off and made ready his side arm; no sense in being too relaxed. As he walked towards David he shouted his name. 'Dave, what's up mate? How the hell did you get here?' Big Dave just stood and watched; Tom was now within ten feet of Big Dave and was starting to feel a little nervous. Why was Dave being this odd?

'You have to stop what you are doing, Tom.' The tone was a matter-of-fact and quite calm.

'We aren't doing anything, Dave; we are waiting to be pulled out.'

Big Dave took a step forward. Oliver had his M4 in the aim and immediately let go with three aimed shots. The angle was good; the bullets went past Tom's left shoulder and impacted in the centre of David's chest; or at least they should have but there was no effect at the target end; David continued to move towards Tom who looked like he was rooted to the spot. It was all over in a split second; Tom said something to Big Dave as he was touched by the bigger man. The outline of Tom gave a brief shimmer than he was gone. Oliver fired another three rounds but the target was now also gone. The bullets impacted on the wall just behind where David had been.

The three men had been surprised how quickly it all happened. The sound of Oliver's weapon firing had got them all moving; all three now reacting as they had all been trained when in a fire fight. Except they were not in a fire fight; there was no incoming and only a single man who appeared to be bullet proof as enemy. Now Tom and Dave were gone.

'Why do you think you missed, Oliver?' Billy was concerned that his brother was displaying an error of judgment.

'I didn't miss; it was a simple shot and all six were on target; no doubt about that. Big Dave should be on the floor over there and very dead.'

Joe was now keying into his Pinger. 'Well we cocked that one up didn't we; remember what we were told? The EDW is the weapon of choice from now on. I have asked for extraction so with any luck we can get out of here soon. Oliver, stand here so you can cover us and don't get too close to anything that will hide Big Dave. Billy and I will see if anything remains of Tom.'

They searched the immediate area and found nothing.

'This is a little curious, Joe.' Oliver was examining the wall that the bullets had hit.

'There are only three impacts on here. I fired six and I can tell you they were all going to the same place. Three of them, and I would suggest the first three, have been intercepted.'

Joe didn't like this one bit and just wanted out. 'The objects did a similar thing if you remember; they looked like they had the ability to turn anything into dust if it was thrown against them; maybe Big Dave is able to do the same thing but what is more worrying is Tom.'

The three men moved off towards the chapel, keeping an eye out for any sign of Big Dave; none of them knew what they would do if he actually returned. There was no sign of David during the short journey back to the chapel; once there they set up a defensive position just outside the main door. Joe did consider going inside but decided against it as they would be blind to any approach from the town.

As they settled down to wait for the helicopter Joe saw Big Dave appear round the side of the nearest house, about fifty metres away. Big Dave strode towards them but stopped just short of the edge of the road.

'Heads up,' Joe said as he caught the movement when Dave returned.

'What is he waiting for?' Oliver was estimating the range and the chances of a first round hit; it looked good as he sighted his M4 and adjusted the sight.

'OK so I know I hit him at least three times in the upper torso but he didn't go down or show any effects; perhaps he is wearing some clever body armour. What do you reckon, Joe?'

Joe was thinking hard; he didn't want to shoot someone he had known on and off for years but Big Dave was not a close acquaintance and he had probably killed his friend.

'Single shot to his head; he doesn't have anything in front of him and we can see his features clear enough.'

Oliver didn't wait for confirmation and fired a single shot that should have gone into David's face just above the centre of his nose. Bang: nothing happened. David just stood in place and didn't move at all.

'Are you sure you hit him?' Joe was also sure Oliver had hit him; the shot could have hardly missed at this range. Oliver squeezed off two more shots with the same effect. Big Dave was still standing looking at them.

Billy ran towards Dave, bringing his EDW into the aim; as he got within twenty feet he fired the device. Big Dave was taken by surprise and stepped back as the discharge hit him but the result was the same as in previous occasions; David was gone with not a trace left.

'What do we make of that then?' All three knew what to make of it; the EDW did work and was able to stop David and the objects that they had encountered previously. The real question was what they would do now. They were still out in the sticks and the chopper was not yet on task.

'The chopper will be here in twenty minutes so I suggest we power up the EDW and be ready for Big Dave if he shows again.' Oliver was looking at the indicators on his weapon.

'Good to go,' Oliver said.

'Roger, fifteen minutes and we are out of here,' Joe said looking at the Pinger again.

David Smith knew he could not let them leave; they had to lead him into the chapel so that the control could be removed. He didn't know why he was doing this but was sure that he had to; he had no choice.

The Blackhawk was making a circuit to check the surrounding area was safe before the pilot committed to landing; no sense at all in putting the aircraft and the two crewmen in danger when they didn't need to. The pilot came around, turned into the wind and reduced the forward speed; he could see the three men moving out towards him from the chapel doorway. As the helicopter contacted the floor the second pilot said something over the intercom that the pilot didn't catch; he turned to look at the other pilot and was startled by what he saw. The other pilot was gone and in his place was a very large man without a flying helmet. The man smiled at him and then reached out to touch his hand. The pilot was not aware of anything else; the whole world seemed to get fuzzy then nothing but blackness.

Joe and the two men were running with heads down towards the Blackhawk when the whole aircraft dissolved;

small particles moving away on the slight breeze. The three stopped, not understanding how this could have happened. The chopper was gone with nothing left in its place; an empty area of ground as if the chopper was never there. 'Back to the chapel, quick as you like; keep your eyes open.'

'Haven't a clue what went on there, fellas; maybe Dave has been at work again.' Joe was hoping for some sort of explanation but didn't think he would get any.

Billy was leaning against the wall of the chapel. 'What is going on? Dave said we were to stop and now we are not allowed to leave; don't get it.'

'The stuff we got from the professor said that the only thing Big Dave said was that we or anyone is to stop what we are doing. Since we aren't doing anything and only wanted to leave I think David has a problem.' Joe was running through in his head exactly what they had done since they had arrived in Ethiopia. They had arrived, found the cylinder and tried to remove it but had dumped it somewhere between here and Asosa then destroyed it. They had then come here and been inside the chapel and Billy had had his chat with the old guy. They hadn't done anything else except try and leave. He was missing something.

'Did anyone see Big Dave out by the chopper?' Oliver was asking the obvious question; none had seen anything except that Blackhawk had briefly touched down and then was gone; it had not flown away.

'You should come this way,' A voice from behind them startled them; it was the old man, speaking English at the first instance this time. *Maybe it's because we are return visitors*, Oliver thought.

They found themselves inside the entrance way of the chapel exactly as they had been before except that Tom was not there.

'What is going on, old man?' Joe didn't really think he would get the answer from the monk but he asked anyway.

'You three are in danger but not only you, the whole of mankind is on the edge of extinction.'

'How do you work that one out?' Oliver sounded more aggressive than he had intended.

'I and the monks before me have been waiting for this time to come; now it is here as predicted. This place is special and is the reason the Ark was brought here; it is the only place that it can be safeguarded from what is outside.'

25.

The old man led them into a corner of the chapel and invited them to sit. There was a long, very old table with a water pitcher and some fruit; there were also some wooden benches that ran either side of the table. All this furniture looked like they had been made a hundred years before; the fruit was very fresh and the water clear.

'None of this was here when we searched this place; they must have a secret storeroom in case they receive visitors.' Oliver was joking of course but he was correct in saying the table and chairs were not present a short time ago.

'Your friend is outside but do not fear you are safe for the present; please eat and quench your thirst.' The old man indicated they should sit and then sat at the end of the table and regarded them one at a time.

'You know about Big Dave?' Joe was not that surprised that the old man had some idea what was going on; he had seemed to know what they were after the last time they were here.

'Your friend David is not the first of his kind to come here; over the centuries men like him have attempted on many occasions to enter this building and the buildings before it.'

'Were they all after the Ark?' Oliver was not convinced about the way the story was going.

'No, not the Ark but the place where the Ark has resided since it was brought here a hundred generations ago. Even that time span shrinks into insignificance when compared with the struggle that mankind had had with the army that David represents.'

'But what significance does the Ark have in relation to this place and Big Dave outside?' Joe thought that this could go on for some time.

'I'm sure you all agree that there are two opposing forces on this world: one of good and one of evil; the distinction is sometimes blurred but the distinction remains all the same. The Ark is here as an arbiter between these two forces; it is also here to maintain the progression of man; without it mankind would cease to progress and would wither and die.'

'So the cylinders and the odd goings-on with Dave are happening to destroy the world?' Billy thought it was turning out to be a simple them-and-us fight.

'No, the world will not be destroyed but will endure; what will be destroyed and removed is mankind as it exists today.'

'But why is mankind being removed?' Joe thought that this would be an interesting report back to the professor; that's if the professor didn't think Joe had lost the plot.

'The Earth is not just a large piece of rock that floats in the void: the Earth is alive and a living entity that grows and will eventually die like all things that are alive.'

The old man watched them; they would not fully understand what he was about to say but he felt that he must say it.

'The Earth is alive and has been alive since the beginnings in the distant past; mankind is but a recent passenger on this planet. Man is part of the current awareness but is not essential and will not endure. Throughout the past there have been many types of being that have inhabited this world but all have adhered to the rules for life. Some of this life have been further advanced than mankind and have prospered. Mankind has prospered but has not remained in control. Man has altered the environment more than can be allowed; he has circumvented the controls that were put in place.'

'So you are part of all this?' Joe was surprised the old man had gone from talking about the cylinders and David to explaining what was to happen and why.

'No, not at all; I am no more a part of what is to happen than you are. The things that are happening now and will happen in the future do not concern me; I am the guardian of the Ark but because I am a man I am part of the problem.'

The old man could see they were not convinced.

'At the beginning of time the Earth was formed and life eventually flourished. As you know the variety of life here is extensive but occasionally one or more types of life become dominant; at the moment mankind is dominant here. It has not always been so; twice in the past a species has become dominant and then become out of control, endangering the very fabric of all life. These have been dealt with in the pre-planned way by the watchers. These are the ones that control and administer the Earth; remember what I said earlier about the Earth being a living thing? Well no part of life here can be allowed to endanger the whole. Now we are here in this time, mankind has to be reset or the whole will die. The watchers, your friend and the cylinders are here to reset; the Earth can only then continue in the manner that was planned.'

'So you are telling us that the Ark is playing some kind of role in this and is a bulwark against the changes that are in progress?' Oliver was still not sure what the Ark was doing in the conversation; he was even starting to believe the Ark existed.

'What will be reset and how can we stop it?' Joe was already sending back a preliminary briefing to the professor;

he was not sure what anyone at the other end would make of this entire ramble. The professor acknowledged his report but didn't comment or ask for anything else. *Perhaps he's busy,* he thought.

The old man smiled. 'It cannot be stopped unless the door is closed.'

'What door? This door?' Oliver indicated the door through which they had entered.

'No, not that door, if only it were that simple. That door will be breached by your friend but by then we will be gone from this room unless of course you wish to face him again.'

'Not at present, old man, but we may have to eventually.' Joe had finished with the report to the professor and had got up.

'If we are not to be here when David comes in where are we going?'

The old man got up and motioned for them to follow; he walked to the rear of the chapel and pulled a large piece of cloth aside that was hanging from the wall; behind it was the door that he and Billy had entered hours before.

'That's odd, the door was over there before.' Billy pointed to a part of the wall about ten feet away.

'Madder by the minute – let's go with it anyway.' Joe followed the old man.

The door opened and the old man entered followed by the three men. The corridor was the same; quite dark and narrow. They were soon in the room at the end of the passage; a room that couldn't possibly be where it was; Joe estimated that they should be about twenty metres beyond where the outside wall should be. Joe thought that this was quite amazing but was starting to get used to the really weird.

The old man motioned for them to step onto the raised platform that was in the middle of the room; a step of about six inches, which Oliver managed to trip over.

'It's so bright in here I didn't see it,' Oliver joked.

The old man was the last to stand on the platform and as he did so the light increased in intensity until it was very difficult to see anything; the light was coming from all directions and not from a single source. The walls shimmered and then appeared to dissolve in the same way people and the helicopter had. As the three men looked into the distance they could see the outside of the chapel; as they took it all in the buildings outside became visible then disappeared in the same shimmer as before. It was perhaps a couple of seconds before they could see the hills in the distance with nothing between them and the horizon. All three turned around and gazed at the view; in all directions there was nothing except the sky and earth; no buildings or structures of any kind.

'That's clever,' Billy said looking at Joe. 'I wonder what sort of CGI this is; it would make a nice home cinema.'

'It is not an illusion.' The old man was looking at them and didn't seem to be very interested in the view that had somehow materialised. 'This is what the land would look like if man had not appeared; if you look closely you will see all manner of life that would have inhabited this area but man is not present.'

'No men? Then what is that?' Oliver pointed to a single figure who was about thirty metres away in the direction the chapel door would have been if it was still there.

The old man looked at the figure and a small frown passed over his face.

'That is your friend but he is not a man any longer; he is watching us but we are safe here for now.'

The old man stepped from the raised platform and the image faded and was replaced by the walls of the chapel.

'Billy, isn't the Ark supposed to be in here?' Joe was looking around the room, which was empty apart from the four men.

'Only the old man is allowed to see the Ark, so it is here

and we can't see it because we are not allowed to or it isn't here and never has been; difficult choice of options I would say.' Billy was now unsure if the Ark was there or not.

'You three must leave here and return to the ship that is waiting for you; you must report to the professor about what you have seen but before you can do that your friend must be removed; if you do not he will kill you.'

The old man turned and motioned for them to follow him; the door opened and they all filed through. Once outside the old man suddenly looked a couple of hundred years older than he had before.

'You must take this.' The old man offered a box to Billy; it was about nine inches square and about six inches deep; it was a very plain wooden box and looked very old. It didn't seem to have a lid or any way of getting into it. On the top a metal disk about two inches in diameter was inlaid into the wood.

'What is it?' Billy asked, quite sure the old man wasn't going to tell him.

'Take it to the professor so he can use it to close the door; only the professor will understand what to do.'

'Hang on, how do you know about the professor? How do you know that this box will help and what is in the box anyway.' Joe was puzzled.

'You three did not happen by this place by chance; if you remember the professor instructed the four of you to come here and seek the Ark. In the end you have arrived here and have indeed found the Ark. It is now time for the three of you to take this to the professor; he will know what to do. Take it!'

Billy took it from the old man; it was surprisingly light and probably weighed half a pound at most.

'What about Big Dave outside?' All three had David in the forefront of their minds and were not looking forward to confronting him again.

The old man spoke. 'Your friend cannot harm you as long as you are close to this.' He touched the box that Billy was holding; his hand rested for some seconds on the surface of the top. The old man looked sad as if he didn't want the box to leave.

As the three men went through the door to the outside Oliver turned and looked at the old man meaning to say thanks and goodbye. The old man was sitting on a small bench that wasn't there when they were talking to him a moment before. He now looked even older and if Oliver had to describe the saddest face he had ever seen then this was it. As Oliver watched the old man he started to fall to pieces as if made from sand; soon there was nothing but dust cascading from the bench onto the floor: the old man was gone.

The three men stood in front of the chapel; Big Dave was looking at them about from thirty metres away.

'I have an idea.' Billy walked forward holding the box in front of him; when he got within range of the EDW he adjusted his grasp on the box so he could point the weapon at Dave. Big Dave didn't move. Billy raised his arm and squeezed the firing device; the electrical discharge arced towards Big Dave and impacted in the centre of his chest. A look of deep sorrow played across David's face; he raised his right arm towards Billy and then was gone.

'That wasn't the same as previous times; he didn't move or avoid the discharge at all; he even stayed there while the contact was made.' Joe was comparing what had happened with what he had thought would happen. Joe typed into the Pinger on his arm. 'Thirty minutes and we are out of here; eyes and ears gentlemen.'

The three men didn't go to the spot where David had been and kept an all-round watch to see if he would return; he didn't and the Blackhawk arrived in a cloud of dust after a twenty-five-minute wait. Joe and Oliver made sure they were not too far away from Billy; whatever it was, or contained, the box seemed to work.

The helicopter lifted off and flew north-west, keeping low until it was well clear of the town. It would be around an hour before they would reach the coast and another twenty minutes before making the carrier.

26.

Within minutes of landing on the *Ronald Reagan* the three men were in the conference room; Billy was still holding onto the box as the professor, the colonel and Lily entered the room.

'What have we here?' The professor was looking at the box that sat on Billy's lap. 'OK, Joe, before we go on, can you fill us in on the detail of what you and your team have been up to?'

Joe told the story from when they were first deployed to Asosa and the search for the cylinder. Of course, the team on the carrier already knew the outline because of the reports that Joe had returned using the Pinger but they were now able to question the players in this particular series of events. Joe explained why the cylinder had to be jettisoned and the detail of Tom's disappearance in Aksum.

'Was there no trace of Tom at all?' Lily asked.

'No, none, nothing at all; he was there one minute then he was gone.'

Joe went on to set out what had happened in the chapel and the room where the Ark was supposed to be.

The professor mulled it over for a few minutes. 'So this old man knew of me and said that the only way to stop whatever is happening was to close the door?'

'Yes, that is about it and Billy here still has the box.'

The professor touched the surface of the box. 'You know,

this is familiar but I cannot put a link to it. I'm sure I have seen it before but I am also very sure that I haven't.'

The professor touched the metal disk that was set into the top of the box; he suddenly twitched and tried to lift his hand; it wouldn't respond, instead his hand dipped into the surface of the box and disappeared into it. The professor's eyes rolled back into his head and he fainted.

The colonel was quickest in the room; he caught the professor before he could fall and lowered him onto the ground. As the professor fell his hand came free of the box but the top seemed to be completely undamaged; there was no indication that his hand had been inside. As soon as he was on the floor the professor regained consciousness.

'My, that was something!'

Billy ran his hand over the disk and prodded it twice but nothing happened; just a box with a metal disk on the top.

'Do you feel OK, professor? Shall we call a medic to have a look at you?' Lily was concerned that something had happened when the professor touched the box and seemed to be the only one in the room that had noticed his hand disappear into the top.

'We need to talk about this, now!' The professor got up and walked to the table at the front of the room. 'Billy, keep a close hold of that box!'

The projector came on; the professor called up the map of the Aksum and zoomed the image in to the area that the chapel was.

'Right then, this is where the Ark of the Covenant is supposed to be, all depending on what sort of faith you follow. The Ark is watched over by a monk who is the only one who is permitted to look upon it; when he dies another monk takes his place and so on. We know that this area is a magnetic anomaly where the normal changes in the Earth's field are not felt; we also know that the cylinders are connected somehow to this magnetic anomaly. David Smith did not seem capable of entering the immediate area of the chapel; why was that? The old man said that this will not stop until the door is closed. Any ideas? No?'

The rest of the room were a little puzzled and did not have the first clue as to what was going on.

The professor went over to the telephone that was linked to the master control room. 'We must proceed to the extraction point as soon as we can, commander… Yes I will, thank you.' The professor put the phone down and sat on the front row of seats. There was an increase in the background vibration as the *Ronald Reagan* ran up to full speed.

It was over an hour before the professor stood up; all in the room were getting a little concerned about his behaviour; he had been sitting staring into to space and occasionally shutting his eyes for minutes at a time as if thinking hard.

'Gentlemen, we are about to hatch a plan but first I must bring someone else into the discussion. He isn't here but I can get him on the link; I will arrange that but, in the meantime, please feel free to get cleaned up and have a bite to eat.' The professor left the room.

The room was silent; only Joe, Billy, Oliver, Lily and the colonel were there.

'Well at least the professor has a plan; I'm very glad no one has asked me for one as I haven't a clue.' Oliver spoke for them all; even the colonel was a little bemused by it all.

'Let's do what the man said. It may get busy from now on. We are making best speed to the extraction point so some of us may not be on *Ronald Reagan* for very much longer.' The colonel went over to the food that was already laid out at the edge of the room when they came in; not stale yet but getting there.

It was two hours before the professor returned; it would be getting dark outside as the carrier raced south.

'Please be seated.' The professor had a bundle of paperwork under his arm and a box containing a disc and several USB sticks; he turned the projector on and sorted through the file system that was displayed. He found the file he was looking for and double-clicked it; on the screen an image appeared of what looked like prehistoric cave painting, the same or similar to the ones that had been found in Southern France over the years.

'Recognise anything in this picture?' The professor looked over his reading glasses at the five sat on the front row; no one answered.

'Cave paintings,' Oliver offered.

'Yes, indeed; cave paintings in a small place in central France you may have heard of, a town called Lascaux. A large amount of such paintings were discovered immediately before World War Two and were opened to the public for a number of years after the war but not so recently as the paintings were deteriorating due to the large amount of visitors. Instead, today the paintings can be viewed in a purpose-built building that houses replicas of the images. Quite interesting should you ever want to go there.'

Several different images flashed onto the screen; about ten in all, each image stayed for about five seconds.

'Still not seeing it? It is in all the images so far. The first ones you saw are about eighteen thousand years old, give or take five hundred years, the later ones are even older. The thing that gets them together, however, is not that they were drawn by prehistoric man but they all contain a single image, or a variation of that image. They are geographically separated by thousands of miles and thousands of years in time so we can safely rule out that the image we are interested in is by the same hand.'

'What image, professor? I saw only animals and some abstract stuff like paint blown over a hand; all things we have seen before at school.'

The first image was back. 'Let me zoom in a little to this point just behind the antelope.'

'Amazing!' Lily was not the only one who was surprised.

The wall of the cave was quite irregular so the drawing of the antelope followed the contours of the rock, giving an almost three-dimensional impression; at the rear of the image was another small drawing, much smaller than the main image. It was a small cylinder shaped representation.

'This is about two inches long by an inch high and is very faint. The imagery here has been enhanced. It is thought that this drawing predates the main animal ones by at least ten thousand years.'

'Could be just a bad drawing of something or not a drawing at all; we humans see faces and things in all manner of situations; remember the face on Mars? Not a face at all but a trick of the light and the contours of the ground. Religious faces appear in fruit and wood all the time.' Joe was saying what most thought; just because it looked like a prehistoric drawing of one of the cylinders does not make it so.

'We do know that the cylinders have been around for much longer than this drawing because we have found evidence, not only here on Earth, but also on Mars and in orbit around Venus. But – and it is a significant but – we now have evidence to show that man has been aware of them since prehistory.'

The slide show continued and on each image the professor pointed out the same representation of the cylinder; all were very small compared with the main imagery.

At the last slide the professor paused. 'Anything else jump out at you?'

The image enlarged and zoomed to the bottom right of

where the cylinder was. A very faint square object with a circle drawn in the centre of what could have been the top of a box. 'It gets better.' The professor changed the aspect of the image; the box seemed to become three-dimensional as the view rotated.

The five people at the front were amazed at the changing shape of the box.

'What does this mean, professor? Does it mean that the artist was aware of perspective or is it just chance?' Lily thought that it was quite a neat drawing but thought that they shouldn't be drawn into seeing things that were not there.

'Most of the cave drawings are two-dimensional and do not appear 3D in most cases. However, some do as the skill of the artist improved. Remember we see depth in photographs because our brains interpret the image from two-dimensional to three. A photograph is on a flat piece of paper but we can still see that the image represents three dimensions – perspective and all that.'

The image changed to one that they had not seen before; it was the same square object but was much more vibrant in colour and definition. The professor moved the image around in the same way he had before. The result was startling; the box was now clearly defined and seemed to move out of the image. 'This is how the image would have appeared when it was originally drawn; good or what!'

All five in the audience were talking about what they had just seen; they were also puzzled about what all this had to do with the plan that was to unfold. Ancient drawings on a cave wall were not going to help them in dealing with the current threat.

'Lily, gentlemen, please be patient.' The picture changed again to the second image that he had been shown a moment before. This time the picture of the box was probably smaller than the first but this was also very different. The room was silent as they looked at the screen. The box was the same proportion as the first but the disc on what could have been the top was not there; instead what appeared to be a hand reaching into it; the finger tips were not shown but the rest of the hand and some of the forearm was quite clear. Billy held the box even tighter.

'This has been noted in three of the ten pictures that I have shown you; a hand that seems to go into the top of a box that does not open. When the hand is not there the disc is present. Anyone seen this before?'

The group were silent, none of them quite sure were this was going.

'Billy, please bring the box over here and place it on the table; do not let go of it. Lily, please come here and push your hand onto the top of the box for me.'

Lily got up and stepped over to the table; she pushed her right hand onto the top but nothing happened.

'Now you, Billy; do not take your other hand from the box.'

Billy had the same result; nothing happened as if he were pushing against the table. The remaining members of the group all did the same with the same result: just a box with a disc inset into the top. Lastly the professor moved forward and pushed his right hand against the top of the box; it appeared to pass right through the disc and into the box; this time the professor didn't faint. The professor withdrew his hand.

'It seems that this box has been known for thousands of years; it is mentioned in numerous texts throughout Europe and the Far East; as you have seen it has even been drawn onto ancient cave paintings.' The professor was waiting for questions.

'Is this the Ark of the Covenant, professor?'

'We don't think so, Lily. More likely the Ark, if it still exists, was placed near this item because of the power it exudes. Remember the electromagnetic anomaly that surrounded the chapel at Aksum? Well that anomaly is now here; so either it came with you individuals or it came with the box. More likely with the box, don't you think?'

'We now have to decide what, if anything, we are to do with it. The team believes that the old man gave it to Billy for a reason; why he chose Billy over anyone else is a mystery. We are not even sure what the old man actually was; as you said he didn't hang around after you left the chapel and you have said the first time you encountered him he was not real but a projection; perhaps he was always a projection. We do not know.'

'You also said that the old man said the Ark was the arbiter between good and evil; are we good or evil? Depends on your point of view, of course.'

'There is a reference to something similar that happened around two thousand BC in northern China.'

The professor explained that some ancient Chinese texts referred to a wooden box that was the key to open or close the door.

'What the door was is not clear but it was hinted that the door was to the heavens. When I put my hand into the box I feel nothing solid; there is nothing that I can feel with my fingers but I do feel a very strong emotional dread and as you saw this was initially overwhelming.' The professor put his hand into the box again. 'The dread is less than before but I can tell you it is not a pleasant feeling.' His hand came out.

Joe was looking closely at the box as the professor's hand went in then came out; there was no movement of the top of the box at all; as the professor's hand went in it was if the wooden top and the flesh of his hand were one.

'So here we have a magic box that only I can get into; the box is special and contains, or is, the key to the heavens. The old man thought it important that it be carried here to me by Billy. In the old text and the cave paintings, we are given no information of where and how it can be used. The door that has been mentioned did generate some thoughts; is the door the anomaly outside of the Moon's orbit through which the cylinders come? If that is the case then the box has been here a very long time without the means to deliver it to the door. Perhaps that is all part of the plan and the box has been passed down through time as a sort of ancestral or genetic memory. There has been some considerable research into the phenomenon of knowing things we didn't learn but the jury is still out on that one.'

The group discussed the options into the night but came to no real conclusions as to what it all meant. The meeting ended at midnight; they were all tired and agreed that it would be better to resume in the morning.

The *Ronald Reagan* had made good time; in about two days they would be at the extraction point and ready for the next phase.

27.

Professor Bobb did not sleep soundly; every couple of minutes he was awoken by strange images and voices in his head. At first he thought that he was having a recurring nightmare but soon realised that it had more substance than that. By the morning he was sure what he had to do; the box wasn't the key to the door but was a way to make the door close; not a key in the sense of the word. The box did not have to go to the anomaly it wasn't designed that way. How did he know all this? The only thing the professor was sure about is that he didn't know.

Billy had slept very well even though he had the box next to him all night; it was jammed between him and the bulkhead so that it was touching him all the time. He was now in the conference room drinking coffee; all the team were there except the professor, who was late, which was unusual for the professor.

The door opened and the professor virtually skipped in to the room; he was very happy and was smiling like the proverbial Cheshire cat. 'All is solved. I know exactly what to do about Billy's box.'

'It is not "my" box!' Billy said under his breath but loud enough for all in the room to hear.

'No, Billy, it is not your box, but you have been chosen to

watch over it for now; in the past, some have watched over it for the most of their lives; some, like you, only have to be the custodian for a few days. All your predecessors have only been the keeper of it and none have been able to unlock its power. That privilege has been carried out by others who have not been great in number; only three until now, I am number four it seems.'

'How do you know that, professor?' Lily was surprised at the professor's attitude; he was normally very subdued and serious; now he had the manner of someone who had won the lottery.

'Lily, my dear friend; we are on the brink of bringing all this to an end; somehow I know exactly what we have to do. I have already informed the committee what we are to do and they are going to assist when we request it.'

'OK, boss, what are we to do?' Even Oliver was being relaxed.

'Oliver, my dear friend.' *Two dear friends,* Joe thought. 'We are about to stop this thing in its tracks, I now know what it is trying to do and why and how we have to put an end to it. Let me tell you; the cylinders do come from the anomaly outside the Moon's orbit; they haven't been coming on a regular basis but have arrived only when the ecosystem on the Earth has required adjustment. Every big change in the structure of the wildlife here has been triggered by the cylinders. Even at the dawn of life they changed the forward march of microbes and changed the direction that evolution was going. Much later on we all learned at school that dinosaurs suddenly disappeared and were replaced by mammals in the pecking order.'

'I thought it was generally accepted that the demise of the dinosaurs was a result of a large asteroid impact, which generated a sudden shift in the climate.' Oliver had always been interested in dinosaurs.

'The asteroid did happen, Oliver, but the day of the dinosaur was already coming to a close; the impact did not have any appreciable effect on the outcome.

'As you may appreciate many species of animal have risen and declined on this planet over the millennia but only mankind has been able to manipulate and change the environment to any great degree. We now have about a hundred times more people on Earth than should be here. We don't lose any significant amount to disease or natural disasters we don't even lose any appreciable amount to war. The natural progression of life on Earth has been changed by a single species: us. Mankind has been chosen for removal from the order of life here: it is either removal or the life on Earth will not endure. There is a plan for life here and mankind is not part of it.'

'Let me get this straight, professor; the cylinders are part of this mechanism to rid the Earth of mankind because "we" are destroying the life on the planet. If we stop this then presumably we will let mankind carry on to destruction; if we don't stop this we will be removed anyway.' Joe was now wondering how they were now in a no-win situation; it had looked promising at the start of the meeting.

'We have two options, Joe and they do not both lead to the same end. One route is certain to remove man from Earth; the other "may" remove mankind. I think that you, as do I, will not want to become a turkey voting for Christmas, so I propose that we close the door and stop the cylinders arriving. Mankind can then go on its way and change its behaviour before the cylinders return. Of course, they may never return but we will be left alone so we can destroy all around us or move in a different direction.'

'If we stop this happening how is the whole of mankind going to change its ways? At this stage very few people even know what is going on.' Joe was having doubts.

'You are correct, of course; the way mankind has traditionally worked together leaves us with grave concerns that there is no solution if it is left to the natural order but it is either that or nothing.'

The control device on the table beeped once. The professor pressed a few keys and a graph appeared on screen. It showed peaks and troughs over a two-day period.

'This is the latest from October. Lily, your team have been very attentive it seems.' The professor indicated the first trough in the readings. 'Have a look at this and note the time at the bottom; this was when I first touched the box and had my hand inside – remember it wasn't pleasant. This one is the second time I did it, although unpleasant, I did not fall over. October has been monitoring the magnetic changes in the overall magnetic field. It seems that the box has an effect on the field; how it does this is a mystery. It would require immense power output to do this so the change is not being driven from the box but I believe the box is the trigger. With a little luck October will be able to locate the epicentre of the power output so we can deliver the box to it.'

The colonel was called from outside; he excused himself and left the room. Lily was called to assist her team on the October project and also left. Only the three-man team and the professor remained.

The professor sat down with the three men. 'Gentlemen, I do not know how all this is working but I appear to be getting little insights about all of this as I am talking to you; it must be something to do with the experience I have had with the box but I am extremely fearful of putting my hand into the box again. Illogical, I know, but there it is. What I propose is that one of you be in contact with me directly as I put my hand in; one of you can hold my hand so to speak.'

Oliver moved forward. 'Right oh, let's do it.'

'Billy, put the box onto the table again but do not lose contact with it.'

Once the box was on the table Oliver grasped the professor's left hand as he put his right hand into the box; the professor closed his eyes but left his hand inside. He kept his hand in for a full minute; much longer than he had before. He didn't seem to be affected by the experience. The professor removed his hand and Oliver let go of the other; Joe and Billy were looking at them.

'Well? What news, professor, Oliver?'

'Didn't feel a thing, nothing at all.' Oliver sounded relieved.

The professor looked at them with an expression that could only be described as sad; it reminded Oliver of the face of the old man as they left.

'I know where this box is to be delivered and we must hurry.' The professor walked out of the room leaving the three men a little puzzled.

'Coffee time,' Joe said and walked over to the side table and poured himself one. 'Anyone else?'

Billy walked over with the box under his arm. 'Yes, I'll have a tea.'

An hour later the professor returned with Lily and the colonel.

'Gentlemen, Lily and her team have confirmed what I suddenly knew when I put my hand in the box; the place we are to place the box is quite close to our present position and easily within helicopter range. The colonel has organised the transport and we will be leaving in about twenty minutes. Billy, Oliver, Joe and I will be taking the box to its final resting place.'

The four men said goodbye to Lily and the colonel and were soon up on the flight deck where a Blackhawk was waiting, rotor turning and ready to go. There were the usual two crew members on board. As soon as they were seated in the rear of the aircraft it took off and flew out into the darkness.

Joe was concerned; he had been on many missions before where he didn't know exactly where and why he was going but this one was now getting into the completely absurd category. *Don't worry, get on with it.* He wondered if the professor had recently thought about the Pandora's box fable; hopefully this was not a Pandora's box that Billy held tightly under his arm.

'We are going to this small island out here in the Arabian Sea; we should be there in an hour. When we arrive we put the box down and leave as soon as we can; it will not be a good idea for us to linger there any longer than we must.'

'Why are we four here, professor? Why not you, Billy and the box. What are me and Oliver going to do?'

'Not sure, Joe, but the box wants us four to be the delivery mechanism for it.'

Under command of the UN and now under command of a box! Joe thought. *Still, I have been commended by people with less expertise than a box in the past so maybe this is a step up.*

The helicopter turned and landed in a cloud of dust. The sun was just about to break the horizon. The four men got out and the helicopter left immediately.

'That's good! We are here for the duration then,' Joe said.

'Don't worry, Joe, we are not going to be left here; the chopper will be back directly.'

The island was not big; they could now see the coast from the central point where they had landed. It was probably around twenty metres above sea level at most; not the normal size of an island that could survive the storms that passed this place from time to time, but here it was.

Professor Bobb was standing near a small raised outcrop that was about the centre of the island; he indicated that Billy should put the box down onto the on top of the large stone.

'Don't worry, Billy, you can let go of the box now; it is where it was intended to be.'

As Billy let go of the box the ground gave an almost imperceptible shimmer; as if a minor earthquake was in progress.

'We must go now, the box will do the rest. I don't know how but by now the magnetic field that had been giving us all the problems will have become uniform and will be closing the door; for better or for worse, we are now on a journey that we cannot change.'

The Blackhawk swooped low and landed a short distance away; as the four men climbed aboard a lone figure was standing at the shoreline at the northern edge of the island. He was unnoticed by the people on the helicopter; the man raised an arm.

'I knew you could get it, professor.' Tom would be the guardian for the time it was needed. He walked over and touched the top of the box; the box then his hand followed by the rest of him fell to the ground as dust.

The journey back to the carrier was made in silence; none of the four men had any real idea of what had just occurred; except perhaps the professor who had said that he knew some things but not all. Once they had landed they found themselves in the room that had been office for the last days.

Lily and the colonel were waiting for them and as soon as they had sat down Lily started the briefing.

'As the professor may have told you the box is doing what he thought it would do. Watch as you came to the island and set the box down.' Lily showed a series of feeds that had come from October; it was monitoring the magnetic changes but was also in direct visual contact with the anomaly out in space. The graph showed a sharp increase in the rate of change as the helicopter approached but the magnetic field levelled out and then returned to the historical normal as the box was set down; there was a very even symmetry to all the readouts that were now showing.

'At this time the anomaly has closed; there is no sign that it will return. The magnetic field is showing smaller and smaller changes than has ever been recorded. We have succeeded; unless we are missing something.'

The watchers had observed the whole journey from the aircraft carrier to the small island. 'They have succeeded,' one of them said.

'Yes, the sequence can proceed as intended; with their timescale they will not know anything of it but we have come to the end point, it is fortunate that they were easily manipulated. All the removed can be returned. We have completed here and can now leave.'

'Time for a drink I think. Shame that the US Navy is a dry organisation; we will have to wait until we get ashore for the parties.' The colonel was pleased that this episode had completed successfully; he was not a great fan of these mixed civilian/military operations but all had panned out in the end. Maybe a long vacation somewhere with a lot of snow.

END POINT

The only one that had been removed that was not returned was David Smith; he was lost forever. Tom would be with the box until it was needed again. The professor, Lily, Joe and the two Clapton brothers went their separate ways. It was thought that whatever threat the cylinders presented had gone away. There were major efforts to control the population but all failed and the number of humans on the planet continued to rise towards the unsustainable.

Eventually, little by little, things started to affect the rise in numbers; disease and the lifesaving drugs that suddenly failed to work took its toll. Within a century there were major conflicts all over the planet; people fighting people for the ever-decreasing resources. The carbon dioxide output from mankind increased exponentially during these times. Society broke down completely in some countries and the population started to decrease. It was reasoned that as the population numbers reduced the environment would recover but it didn't; mankind's inexorable slide to extinction had begun.

It took thousands of years for the planet to recover but mankind was no longer present; the magnetic field remained as it was before with only minor changes caused by the activity of the Sun. A new life form appeared in the north of Africa that did show promise but it would be millennia before it would venture from the continent in any numbers.

The small island remained; if and when it was visited Tom would be there to guard over the box until he passed it on.

The watchers had intended that the box was relocated but had failed on many occasions before. This time mankind had moved it, despite the sequence being against them. They would return to oversee the progression.

MEET THE AUTHOR

Can you describe your new novel, *End Point*?

End Point is a science fiction novel set in the present day and centred on the problems that the world is facing. A small group are at the sharp end of a major investigation into why objects are falling to earth. They discover that the objects have been around for some time and have not just been landing on earth.

The team are led on a wild chase from a wet Welsh valley all the way to Ethiopia, where the 'end point' is revealed.

Can you tell us how you came to win the competition to have your book published?

My wife bought me a copy of the *Writing Magazine* last year and said I should enter the competition. I entered and thought nothing more about it until Troubador emailed in the New Year saying I had won and that my book would be published and marketed as part of the prize.

What was your inspiration for the book?

I like books that have an unusual twist. I tried to get away from *the Alien turns up and destroy the world* or *kill all the people* etc.

What do you want readers to take away when they've reached the end of the book?

When people have read *End Point* they may like to think about the way the world and mankind are going. Mankind has control over most of what happens but not all – is there a master plan or is everything random?

Now that your book has been produced as part of your competition prize, does it live up to expectations?

The production of *End Point* is fascinating, very much more involved than I originally thought; the team have been amazing and I am continually impressed by the professionalism shown. The end result will, I am sure, exceed my expectations.

What interests you most about writing?

I have always been interested in making up stories. I used to tell our children and grandchildren stories that I made up on the spot and they always seemed to go down well.

What authors inspire you?

My favourite book is without doubt *On the Beach* by Nevil
Shute. Early Wilber Smith novels were also high on my
reading list.

Which book first gave you the reading bug?

The first book that had me hooked was a children's sci-fi novel
about an alien that kept returning to earth because he liked tea.
He would take a group of small children out into space and
show them around fantastic planets before returning them to
earth. I was probably about ten when I read them and for the
life of me I cannot remember what they were called or who
wrote them. But after I read the whole series several times I
was hooked on adventure and science fiction.

**Are there more books by Peter Breakspear in the
pipeline?**

I am about half way through another novel; again it is science
fiction but this time the action is set by a criminal group who
are trying to manipulate the population. It hasn't got a title as
yet!